Ahmad Usman is a dynamic writer and entrepreneur with a rich background spanning multiple disciplines. Specializing in geopolitics, social issues, and technology, he brings a unique blend of practical and theoretical knowledge to his work. As the Founder & CEO of an innovative startup, Ahmad is making significant strides in space exploration, leveraging his expertise to push the boundaries of what is possible. His journey to the forefront of space technology highlights his adaptability, visionary thinking, and dedication to advancing human knowledge and capabilities. Ahmad's diverse experiences and forward-thinking approach position him as a leading voice in the intersection of technology and societal advancement.

To my beloved parents, whose unwavering love, guidance, and sacrifices have shaped the person I am today, and to my cherished wife, the constant source of strength, inspiration, and love in my life. To my wonderful children, whose boundless curiosity and joy inspire me every day.

Ahmad Usman

ECHOES OF THE UNKNOWN

AUSTIN MACAULEY PUBLISHERS®

LONDON • CAMBRIDGE • NEW YORK • SHARJAH

Ordering Information
Quantity sales: Special discounts are available on quantity purchases by corporations, associations, and others. For details, contact the publisher at the address below.

Publisher's Cataloging-in-Publication data
Usman, Ahmad
Echoes of the Unknown

ISBN 9798891556508 (Paperback)
ISBN 9798891556515 (ePub e-book)

Library of Congress Control Number: 2024918092

www.austinmacauley.com/us

First Published 2024
Austin Macauley Publishers LLC
40 Wall Street, 33rd Floor, Suite 3302
New York, NY 10005
USA

mail-usa@austinmacauley.com
+1 (646) 5125767

Part 1

It was a cold November night, the kind that seemed to seep into your bones, uninvited and unrelenting. I sat alone on a weathered bench on the Brooklyn Bridge, gazing out at the water below. The river, dark and inscrutable, flowed beneath me, its surface a canvas for the moon's mysterious luminescence. The night was colder than the water, yet my heart felt even colder, an icy void within my chest.

As I sat there, my hands tucked into the pockets of my black leather jacket, I couldn't help but reflect on the journey that had led me to this solitary moment. My life replayed in my mind, each memory a wave crashing against the shores of my consciousness.

I was born in the bustling heart of New York, at Bellevue Hospital. My birth was not celebrated; instead, it was a burden. My father, a man more acquainted with the inside of Bronx bars than his own home, was lost to addiction. He drowned his sorrows in cheap beer, leaving my mother to face the harsh realities of life alone.

My mother was a shadow in my life, a presence that was there but never truly with me. Overwhelmed by the responsibilities of a child she never planned for, she handed me over to the only person willing to shoulder the burden—my grandmother.

Grandma Eleanor lived in a small, aging house in Tarrytown, a quiet town that stood in stark contrast to the ceaseless energy of New York City. She was a woman of humble means but possessed a wealth of love and kindness. Although her life had been marred by my grandfather's early death, she never let her hardships define her.

Tarrytown was my sanctuary during those formative years. The streets were lined with old trees that whispered stories of the past, and the people were a tight-knit community who looked out for each other. Grandma Eleanor's house, with its peeling paint and creaking floors, was a testament to her resilience.

She enrolled me in Willow Creek Elementary, a small school that became my haven for learning. It was here, amidst the outdated textbooks and aging computers, that I discovered my passion for technology. I remember the first time I managed to boot up one of the old computers in the library; it was like opening a door to a new world.

But my world shattered when I was eight. Grandma Eleanor passed away, leaving me adrift in a sea of uncertainty. I was taken in by my uncle James and aunt Linda in their home in Scarsdale. Uncle James was a gentle soul who tried his best to provide me with the fatherly guidance I lacked. Aunt Linda, however, was less welcoming. She viewed me as an unwanted responsibility, a sentiment that was never spoken but always felt.

In Scarsdale, I attended Oakwood Middle School, where I continued to foster my love for computers. I was often alone, a solitary figure drifting through the hallways, my mind always elsewhere, lost in algorithms and code. My uncle and aunt's house, though larger and more modern than Grandma Eleanor's, lacked the warmth and love that I had known. It was just a place to sleep, not a home.

The challenges I faced in those years were numerous. Financial constraints meant I couldn't afford the luxuries my classmates took for granted. I watched from the sidelines, an outsider looking in, as they flaunted the latest gadgets and talked about their extravagant holidays. My world was different; it was one of thrift stores and hand-me-downs, of counting pennies and saving every dollar.

But these hardships only fueled my determination. I took on part-time jobs—mowing lawns, delivering newspapers, and tutoring younger students. Each job was a step toward my goal, a badge of my independence and resilience. My dream was to own a computer, a portal to the world I so dearly loved.

It wasn't until high school that my efforts began to bear fruit. I was accepted into the prestigious Hudson High School on a scholarship. The school was a stark contrast to Oakwood, with its state-of-the-art facilities and a student body that oozed privilege. But it was here that my talents in computer science were truly nurtured.

I joined the computer club, participated in coding competitions, and even started a small freelance business, helping local businesses with their IT needs. My nights were spent in the glow of my computer screen, coding, learning, and escaping into a world where I felt in control.

As my time in high school progressed, my fascination with technology became more than just a hobby; it was my lifeline. I found solace in the methodical nature of coding, the way each line built upon the last to create something whole and functioning. It was a stark contrast to the unpredictability of my life.

In the small bedroom at my uncle and aunt's house, I spent countless nights immersed in the glow of my secondhand computer screen. It wasn't much, but to me, it was a gateway to another universe. I learned different programming languages, experimented with software development, and even dabbled in the emerging field of artificial intelligence. The digital world was one where I had control, a stark contrast to the helplessness I felt in my daily life.

My academic prowess did not go unnoticed. Teachers and peers began to recognize my talents, and I was often called upon to assist with various technology-related projects around the school. This recognition was a bittersweet experience for me. On one hand, it was affirming to be acknowledged for my skills, but on the other, it was a constant reminder of my solitary journey.

High school was also a time of profound personal growth. The challenges of living in a household where I felt like an outsider taught me resilience and independence. I learned to navigate the complexities of human relationships, often finding that my analytical mind struggled to decipher the nuances of social interactions.

The isolation I felt at home was mirrored in my social life. I had acquaintances at school, but no one I could truly call a friend. My peers were caught up in their own lives, engrossed in teenage dramas that seemed trivial compared to the struggles I faced. I often felt like an observer, watching the world from a distance, unable to fully engage.

Despite these challenges, I found a sense of purpose in my part-time jobs. Each task, no matter how mundane, was a step toward my independence. I saved every dollar I earned, planning for a future where I could break free from the confines of my current life.

The day I received the scholarship letter from Hudson High was a turning point. It was an acknowledgment of my hard work and a beacon of hope for a better future. The scholarship covered my tuition in full, a relief to my uncle and aunt and a source of immense pride for me.

Hudson High was a world apart from Oakwood. Here, I was surrounded by students who were as driven and ambitious as I was. The competitive environment pushed me to excel, to delve deeper into my studies, especially in computer science.

I remember the first time I won a coding competition. The feeling of triumph was exhilarating, a validation of my skills and hard work. It was moments like these that made the sleepless nights and endless hours of studying worth it.

As senior year approached, the reality of college applications loomed large. I knew that my future depended on getting into a good university, a place where I could continue to pursue my passion for technology. I spent hours researching schools, writing essays, and preparing for interviews.

The pressure was immense. I was not only competing against my classmates but also against students from all over the country. But I was determined to succeed, to break the cycle of hardship that had defined my family for generations.

Finally, the acceptance letters began to arrive. Each one was a confirmation of my abilities and the potential for a brighter future. I was accepted into several prestigious universities, each offering opportunities I had never dared to dream of.

Gaining admission into New York University on a scholarship marked the beginning of a new chapter in my life, a chapter filled with promise and the fulfillment of long-held dreams. This was not just an academic achievement; it was a milestone that signified my escape from the confines of my past and the start of a journey toward independence and self-discovery.

Leaving my uncle and aunt's house in Scarsdale was a bittersweet moment. For years, their home had been a roof over my head—a place of safety, but not of warmth. Now, as I packed my few belongings, I felt a mixture of excitement and apprehension. The life I had known was about to change, and the prospect of living independently in New York City filled me with an exhilarating sense of freedom.

New York City, with its towering skyscrapers and bustling streets, was a far cry from the quiet suburbs of Scarsdale. It was a city that never slept, pulsating with energy and life. I was instantly captivated by its vibrancy and diversity. Here, in this sprawling metropolis, I felt a sense of belonging that had eluded me in the quieter corners of my past.

My new home was a modest hostel apartment in the heart of Manhattan. It was small, but it was mine—a sanctuary where I was the master of my own destiny. The cityscape outside my window was a constant reminder of the infinite possibilities that lay ahead. For the first time in my life, I was truly on my own, responsible for my decisions and my future.

At New York University, I was immersed in an environment that celebrated knowledge and innovation. The university was renowned for its programming and computer science courses, and I found myself surrounded by like-minded individuals who shared my passion for technology. It was a stimulating and challenging environment, one that pushed me to expand my boundaries and explore new horizons.

My programming skills, which I had honed over years of self-learning and experimentation, quickly caught the attention of my professors and peers. I was no longer the overlooked student from a small-town high school. Here, in this prestigious university, my talents were recognized and appreciated. I became involved in various coding projects, collaborating with other students on complex algorithms and software development.

One of the most significant projects I undertook was developing a software program that could optimize data analysis for research purposes. This program caught the attention of one of my professors, who saw its potential for wider application in academic research. Working on this project not only sharpened my coding skills but also taught me the value of technology in facilitating knowledge and innovation.

Outside the classroom, New York City offered a myriad of opportunities to further my learning and experience. I attended tech meetups, hackathons, and guest lectures, each event providing valuable insights into the ever-evolving world of technology. These experiences not only enhanced my technical skills but also helped me build a network of contacts in the industry.

Life in New York was exhilarating and challenging in equal measure. Balancing my academic responsibilities with the demands of independent living was not always easy, but it taught me the importance of resilience and time management. Each day was a learning experience, an opportunity to grow both personally and professionally.

Reflecting on my journey from the uncertainty of my childhood to the bustling streets of New York, I felt a profound sense of achievement. The hardships I had faced, the obstacles I had overcome, had all led me to this point. They had forged me into someone who was not only capable of facing challenges but also thriving in the face of them.

As I walked through the vibrant neighborhoods of Manhattan, I realized that New York was more than just a city to me—it was a symbol of my aspirations and dreams. It was here, amidst the energy and dynamism of the city, that I found my true calling in the world of programming. And as I looked toward the future, I was filled with an unshakable belief in my ability to succeed and make a meaningful impact in the world of technology.

With each passing day, my confidence grew, and my dreams seemed increasingly within reach. New York University was not just an institution of learning; it was a launchpad for my ambitions, a place where I could turn my passion for programming into a purposeful and rewarding career.

Embracing life at New York University and the city itself became a journey of self-discovery and enjoyment for me. Each day was an amalgamation of academic rigor and the vibrant pulse of city life. The sprawling urban landscape of New York, with its endless possibilities, became my playground.

On days when the city was draped in rain, I found a unique solace in wandering its streets. The raindrops created a rhythmic symphony against the sidewalks, and the cold winds whispered secrets of the city's past. These solitary walks were moments of introspection, where I connected with the city on a deeper level. The towering skyscrapers, glistening under the wet sky, stood as monuments to human ingenuity and perseverance.

In between my studies, I indulged in my love for reading. Bookstores dotted around the city became my havens. There, amidst rows of books, I traveled to distant lands and times. Each book was a window into another world, another perspective. It was during these quiet moments, lost in the pages of a novel, that I felt a profound connection with the broader tapestry of human experience.

My social life blossomed as well. I forged friendships with fellow students who shared my interests and passions. We were a diverse group, each bringing our unique stories and backgrounds to the table. Our hangouts were filled with lively discussions, debates, and laughter. We explored the city's eclectic neighborhoods, each outing an adventure in itself. From the historic streets of Greenwich Village to the bustling avenues of Midtown, every corner of New York had a story to tell.

Despite the exhilaration of university life and the allure of the city, thoughts of my family often lingered in the back of my mind. My parents, especially my mother, remained enigmatic figures in my life. My last information about her was that she had left for San Francisco, leaving me behind with my grandmother. I often wondered about her life there, about the choices she had made. These thoughts were accompanied by a complex mix of emotions—curiosity, longing, and a sense of unresolved history.

The stark contrast between my vibrant life in New York and the unknowns of my mother's life in San Francisco created an emotional dichotomy. I contemplated reaching out, yet hesitated, unsure of the reception I would receive. This internal conflict was a reminder of the unresolved threads of my past.

Despite these lingering questions, I was determined not to let them overshadow the life I was building. New York had become my home, a place where I had grown and thrived. My experiences at the university, the friendships I had formed, and the personal growth I had undergone were testament to how far I had come.

As I walked through the city, feeling the rain on my face and the wind in my hair, I realized that this was where my story was unfolding. The city, with its endless energy and possibilities, mirrored my own journey of self-discovery and growth. New York, in all its complexity and vibrancy, was a reflection of my own aspirations and dreams.

In those moments of wandering the rain-soaked streets, I made peace with the uncertainties of my past. I embraced the present, with all its challenges and opportunities. The city, with its unyielding spirit, had taught me the importance of resilience and the beauty of forging one's path.

As I looked toward the future, I knew that whatever it held, I was ready to meet it head-on. The experiences and lessons I had gained in New York had equipped me with the tools to navigate the journey ahead. And as the city lights twinkled in the rain, I felt a deep sense of gratitude for the journey that had brought me here, to this moment, to this place that I now called home.

In my fifth semester at New York University, my path crossed with a remarkable individual, Ava Thompson. Ava, a member of my project group, was a whirlwind of energy and confidence. She was the daughter of the global head of a major tech company, coming from a world of affluence and influence.

From our first meeting, Ava's presence was undeniable. She radiated a kind of vitality that was both inspiring and intimidating. Unlike the typical offspring of the wealthy, Ava wore her privilege with a sense of responsibility and grace. She was not just another student at the university; she was a force to be reckoned with.

Ava's golden hair, which cascaded down her shoulders, seemed to capture the essence of her personality—bright, eye-catching, and full of life. She often wore black glasses, which added a touch of scholarly seriousness to her otherwise vivacious appearance. But it wasn't just her physical attributes that made her stand out. Ava was deeply involved in university life, actively participating in social activities and clubs. As the president of the debate club, she demonstrated not only her eloquence but also her ability to think critically and engage with complex issues.

Despite her many admirable qualities, Ava wasn't what I had envisioned as my 'dream girl'. However, I found myself drawn to her openness and her social nature. She had a way of making everyone around her feel included and valued, a trait that was rare and endearing. Ava's enthusiasm for life was contagious, and her confidence seemed unshakable.

Unlike most students, Ava chose to live alone in a studio apartment in one of New York's more upscale neighborhoods, instead of the university hostel. Her apartment was a reflection of her personality—stylish, organized, and adorned with various artifacts that spoke of her travels and experiences. It was evident that she enjoyed her independence and had a taste for the finer things in life.

Our interactions were mostly limited to group work initially, but as time passed, we found ourselves in deeper conversations about technology, life, and our aspirations. Ava had a keen interest in using technology for social good, and her ideas were often innovative and forward-thinking. Her background in a tech-savvy family had given her insights that were both profound and practical.

Yet, despite her many qualities and the time we spent together, I couldn't shake the feeling that a romantic relationship with Ava wasn't something I yearned for. It wasn't a lack of attraction—Ava was undoubtedly beautiful and charming—but rather an intuitive sense that our paths, though intersecting now, were ultimately headed in different directions.

Ava's approach to life was different from mine. Where I was introspective and often reserved, she was outgoing and effervescent. Her world was one of gala events and high-profile social gatherings, while I found comfort in the quieter, more intimate settings. This contrast in our personalities and lifestyles made me question the possibility of a deeper connection beyond the realms of friendship and professional collaboration.

As the semester progressed, my admiration for Ava as a person and a professional only grew. I respected her for her intellect, her passion for social causes, and her ability to navigate her privileged world with a sense of purpose. However, I remained mindful of the emotional boundaries between us, appreciating the unique friendship we had formed, while acknowledging the unlikelihood of a romantic future together.

In Ava, I saw a mirror reflecting a world vastly different from my own, yet equally intriguing and full of lessons. Our friendship became a valuable part of my life, offering a perspective that was both challenging and enriching. As I navigated my way through the complexities of university life and the broader journey of self-discovery, Ava remained a significant, albeit platonic, presence in my world.

Ava's apartment was located in the trendy neighborhood of Williamsburg, Brooklyn, a place synonymous with artistic flair and an eclectic cultural scene. Our study sessions and occasional social gatherings there were a blend of academic rigor and the casual ease of newfound friendship.

The dynamic between us was an intriguing one. Ava, with her vibrant personality and affluent background, was a stark contrast to my more modest upbringing and introspective nature. Yet, in the realm of academics, particularly in programming and technology, we found common ground. Our sessions were often intense, delving deep into complex algorithms and theoretical concepts, yet they were always imbued with a sense of mutual respect and a shared drive for knowledge.

One particular night, a sense of urgency unexpectedly wove itself into the fabric of our routine. It was a chilly Friday evening in late autumn. The city was alive with its usual nocturnal energy, the streets echoing with the distant sounds of traffic and the occasional laughter spilling out from the neighborhood bars.

I was at my apartment, engrossed in a book, when my phone rang, slicing through the quiet. Ava's name flashed on the screen. Answering the call, I was immediately struck by the unusual tone in her voice. It was tinged with anxiety, a stark departure from her usual confident demeanor.

"I'm really struggling with this machine learning problem," she said, her voice laced with frustration. "I could use your help, if you're free."

I could sense the underlying stress in her request. Ava was not someone to ask for help lightly. She was fiercely independent, often preferring to wrestle with challenges on her own rather than seek assistance. Her reaching out was a clear indication of the seriousness of her predicament.

"Of course. I'll come over," I responded without hesitation. "Just give me an hour or so."

Grabbing my laptop and a few textbooks, I hurried out, locking my door behind me. The night air was crisp, the city's lights reflecting off the low-hanging clouds, giving the sky a luminescent quality. I made my way to the bus stop, the streets quieter than usual, with most of the city's residents enjoying the start of the weekend indoors.

The bus ride to Williamsburg was a journey I had made several times before, but tonight, it felt different. The usual hum of the city seemed to fade into the background as my thoughts centered on Ava and the task that lay ahead. The bus trundled through the streets, its rhythm a steady companion in the quiet of the night.

As the bus crossed the Williamsburg Bridge, I gazed out at the expanse of the East River below, its surface a dark, undulating mass under the city lights. The bridge, a testament to human engineering and perseverance, stood as a metaphor for the journey I was on—a bridge between different worlds, different lives.

My mind wandered to Ava and the world she inhabited. Her life, so different from mine, was a mosaic of privilege and high expectations. Yet, beneath the veneer of affluence and confidence, I had begun to see glimpses of the real Ava—dedicated, vulnerable, and driven by a desire to make a mark in the world.

The bus made its way through the streets of Williamsburg, the neighborhood's unique character on display even in the quiet of the night. Street art adorned the walls of old warehouses, trendy cafes and bars stood side by side with old-school delis, and the eclectic mix of people that called this place home added to its charm.

As the bus neared her apartment, my anticipation grew. I was not just going to help a friend in need; I was stepping into a situation that blurred the lines between academic collaboration and personal connection. Ava and I, in our shared pursuit of knowledge, had formed a bond that was as complex as it was unexpected.

The bus came to a stop, and I disembarked, the cold air greeting me like an old friend. I made my way to her apartment building, the city's soundtrack a faint echo in the background. The night was still young, and the task ahead promised to be challenging, but I was ready. In helping Ava, I was not only offering my expertise but also strengthening a connection that had become an important part of my university life.

As a young man at New York University, I carved out a niche for myself that went beyond academics. Recognized for my striking looks and my accolades in programming and artificial intelligence, I had become somewhat of an enigma on campus. Winning national awards had not only bolstered my reputation but also brought a level of respect and familiarity among my peers and professors alike.

Despite the attention, my focus remained unwavering. The allure of fleeting campus romances never swayed me. I had seen many of my fellow students get lost in the whirlwind of university relationships, only to emerge distracted and off-course. That was not going to be my story. My goals were clear—to excel in my field and to make the most of the opportunities that my scholarship and skills afforded me.

As a freelancer, my projects in programming and AI were not just a means to apply my knowledge but also a significant source of income. The financial independence I gained from these ventures allowed me a certain lifestyle in New York, a city where dreams and indulgences came at a price. I found solace in solitary explorations of the city, wandering through its diverse neighborhoods, each with its unique flavor and story.

New York, with its endless energy and vibrant culture, was the perfect backdrop for my solitary sojourns. I spent my evenings exploring, from the historic streets of Greenwich Village, brimming with artistic heritage, to the bustling avenues of Times Square, ablaze with neon lights and the pulse of the city. These walks were my escape, a way to disconnect from the demands of university life and to connect with the city that had become my home.

My culinary adventures were an integral part of these excursions. New York's gastronomic landscape was a paradise for a food lover like me. From savoring the street food in Hell's Kitchen to indulging in fine dining experiences in upscale Manhattan restaurants, each meal was a journey in itself. These moments of solitude, surrounded by the hum of the city, were when I felt most at peace.

Despite my introverted tendencies, I was not immune to the charms of the city's nightlife. I occasionally found myself in the heart of New York's vibrant party scene. The music, the people, the entire atmosphere was intoxicating, yet I always maintained a certain distance, an observer more than a participant. The night was a time for reflection, for experiencing the city in its truest form, unadulterated and raw.

And so, on that particular night, as I stood in front of Ava's apartment building, these reflections occupied my mind. The journey from my apartment to hers was more than just a physical traverse across the city; it was a transition from my world into hers. Ava, with her dynamic personality and affluent background, represented a different side of New York, one that was as intriguing as it was distant from my own experiences.

As I paused outside her building, taking in the quiet street and the occasional passing car, I realized that this was yet another facet of my life in New York. Here I was, about to step into the world of a friend who had, in her own way, become a part of my journey. The night was still, the city's heartbeat a soft murmur in the background, and as I reached for the door, I left behind my thoughts, ready to immerse myself in the task ahead—helping Ava with her machine learning project. It was moments like these, small intersections of lives and stories, that made my time in New York a tapestry of experiences, each thread weaving into the next, creating a picture that was uniquely mine.

The apartment building where Ava resided was a reflection of her life—polished, upscale, and standing tall amidst the vibrant backdrop of Williamsburg. As I rang the bell, the lateness of the hour weighed on my mind. The city was enveloped in a nocturnal tranquility, broken only by the occasional distant sounds of late-night traffic and the ever-present hum of the city that never sleeps.

When Ava opened the door, the scene before me was unexpected. It was past 1 AM, yet she stood there, a vision in black, wearing a dress that seemed too elegant for the hour. The dress clung to her in all the right places, accentuating her slender frame and the effortless grace she carried herself with. The soft lighting of the hallway cast gentle shadows across her features, enhancing her beauty.

Her eyes, usually so full of confidence and vivacity, held a hint of anxiety, an unusual expression for someone who typically exuded self-assuredness. The sight of her, so out of context in the serene night, added a layer of complexity to the situation.

"Come in," she said, her voice a mixture of warmth and something unreadable. "Let's sit on the balcony."

I stepped into the apartment, my senses immediately inundated with the contrasting atmospheres. The interior was a stark departure from the calm exterior of the building. Books were strewn about in what appeared to be a haphazard manner, papers littered the floor, and the faint glow of her laptop screen illuminated the room with an eerie light. The disarray was uncharacteristic of Ava, known for her meticulousness and organization.

The balcony overlooked the sleeping city, a panoramic view of Williamsburg bathed in the soft glow of the moon and the sporadic twinkling of distant lights. The night air was cool, a gentle breeze wafting through, carrying with it the faintest sounds of the city's nightlife. It was a peaceful setting, a stark contrast to the chaotic interior of the apartment.

Ava disappeared for a moment, leaving me alone with my thoughts on the balcony. The scenario was puzzling. What had started as a call for help with machine learning had transformed into something else entirely, something I couldn't quite put my finger on.

When she returned, she carried two drinks, handing one to me with a smile that didn't quite reach her eyes. Her demeanor was different—there was a playfulness to her actions, a stark contrast to the Ava I knew in the university setting. She seemed to be enjoying my visible confusion, a slight upturn to her lips as she watched me.

I took the drink, my mind still trying to piece together the evening's events. The balcony, with its view and the tranquility it offered, seemed like a world apart from the disordered state of her living room. Ava leaned against the railing, her gaze fixed on the cityscape, yet I could feel her awareness of my presence.

The silence between us was comfortable yet charged with an unspoken question. What was the purpose of this late-night summons? Ava's usual straightforwardness was absent, replaced by an enigma that was both intriguing and disconcerting.

As we stood there, the city beneath us, a sense of surrealism enveloped the moment. The Ava in front of me was a departure from the confident, focused individual I had come to know. This Ava was more elusive, her intentions unclear, her usual candor replaced by a mysterious allure.

The drink in my hand was a welcome distraction, the cool liquid a contrast to the warmth of the night. The balcony, suspended above the sleeping city, felt like a separate realm, a place where the usual rules and expectations didn't apply. Here, in this space, Ava and I were just two individuals, away from the roles we played in the university, away from the eyes of the world.

The situation was a puzzle, one that I found myself increasingly drawn into. Ava's presence, the disarray of her apartment, and the unusual hour—all these elements combined to create a scenario that was as baffling as it was intriguing. As I took a sip of my drink, I let the confusion wash over me, deciding to embrace the unpredictability of the moment. For now, the night was ours, and the city below was our silent witness. In that quiet balcony setting, with the city's lights stretching out beneath us, the atmosphere was thick with unspoken words. Ava's playful demeanor, so different from her usual confident and direct self, added layers to her personality I hadn't seen before. There was an air of mystery about her that night, a departure from the logical, straightforward person I knew.

She leaned over the railing, looking out over Williamsburg, her profile silhouetted against the city lights. The gentle breeze played with her golden hair, occasionally blowing strands across her face. She seemed lost in thought, a stark contrast to the usual clarity and focus she exhibited.

The ambiance on the balcony was a mix of tranquility and subtle tension. The peaceful night and the serene view juxtaposed with the complexity of the situation inside. The clutter of books and papers in her apartment suggested a frantic study session, yet her poised appearance and the late hour painted a different picture.

I couldn't help but feel out of place, like a piece in the wrong puzzle. Ava's invitation, her attire, the disarray inside—none of it made sense in the context of a simple study session. Yet, here I was, trying to navigate through the ambiguity of the situation.

The stillness of the night was only broken by the soft whisper of the breeze and the distant hum of the city. Ava and I stood on her balcony, enveloped in the serene beauty of the moonlit night, the air charged with an undercurrent of unspoken thoughts. The tranquility of the moment was a stark contrast to the turmoil of emotions that Ava's question had stirred within me.

"How am I for you?" she had asked, her voice barely above a whisper, yet it cut through the night with startling clarity. It was a question that seemed to hang in the air, its weight palpable. I was taken aback, not just by the abruptness of the question but by the intensity behind it.

I had always seen Ava as a friend, a fellow student whose company I enjoyed, whose intellect I admired. But love? That was a realm I had consciously steered clear of, focusing instead on my studies and personal growth. The truth was, I did like her. Her vivacity, her passion for life, and her innate kindness had always drawn me to her. But to consider these feelings as anything more than platonic was a territory I hadn't ventured into.

Trying to maintain a semblance of casualness, I replied, "I like you, Ava. Everyone does. You're hard not to like." My words, carefully chosen, were an attempt to deflect the depth of the conversation.

However, Ava was not one to be easily dissuaded. Closing the distance between us, she looked into my eyes, her own reflecting a mix of emotions. "I like you so much, more than anyone else," she confessed, her voice laced with sincerity. "That's why I called you here tonight, to share my feelings with you."

Her admission left me speechless. The Ava I knew was always composed, always in control. But here she was, laying her emotions bare, vulnerable yet resolute. The realization that she saw me as more than just a friend or a study partner was overwhelming.

I could feel my heart racing, a myriad of emotions coursing through me. I was flattered, of course, but also confused and unsure. Ava was an incredible person, and the thought that she felt this way about me was both humbling and disconcerting.

Seeing my discomfort, Ava stepped back, giving me space. "I don't want to pressure you," she said gently. "Take your time to think about it. I just wanted you to know how I feel."

Her words were a balm, calming the storm of thoughts in my mind. Ava was offering me something profound—a chance at a relationship that was beyond the simple confines of friendship. But she was also giving me the freedom to choose, to ponder over what this meant for me, for us.

The night air felt cooler now, the earlier warmth replaced by a subtle chill. I wrapped my arms around myself, trying to process the enormity of what Ava had just revealed. Here, on this balcony, with the city spread out beneath us, my carefully structured world had been gently but irrevocably shaken.

Ava, sensing my need to process everything, suggested we head inside. The apartment, with its disarray of books and papers, seemed like a stark reminder of the reality we both lived in—a world of academics, ambitions, and future aspirations.

We sat in her living room, each lost in our thoughts. The drink she had offered earlier sat forgotten on the coffee table, the ice cubes slowly melting away. The silence between us was comfortable yet filled with unspoken questions and possibilities.

As the night wore on, we talked about everything and nothing. Ava shared more about her life, her dreams, and her fears. She spoke of the pressures of living up to her family's expectations, of her desire to carve her own path in the world. I listened, seeing her in a new light, understanding the complexities of her life.

When it was time for me to leave, the first light of dawn was breaking over the horizon. The city that never slept was slowly waking up, its energy seeping back into the streets. Ava walked me to the door, her demeanor back to its usual confident self, but there was a softness in her eyes that hadn't been there before.

Stepping out into the cool morning air, I felt a sense of uncertainty mixed with a newfound awareness. Ava's confession had opened a door to possibilities I had never considered. The walk back home was a blur, my mind racing with thoughts of Ava, of what her feelings meant for our friendship, and what this could mean for my own carefully laid plans.

As I navigated the quiet streets, the city slowly coming to life around me, I realized that Ava's proposition was not just about a potential romantic relationship. It was an invitation to explore a deeper connection, to consider a partnership that could add a new dimension to my life.

But was I ready for it? Was I willing to venture into the uncharted territory of love?

As I walked toward the bus stop, my mind was a whirlwind of thoughts and emotions. Ava's confession had stirred something within me, a tumult of feelings I couldn't easily categorize or understand. It was true; I had no intention of starting a romantic relationship. My plans were clear, my path well-charted toward personal and professional achievements. Love, especially the profound and all-encompassing kind Ava hinted at, was not a part of that plan.

Yet, as the city passed by in the blur of the bus window, Ava's sincerity and the depth of her feelings were impossible to dismiss. It was flattering, undoubtedly, to be the object of such affection and regard, especially from someone as admirable as Ava. Her confession was not just a declaration of love; it was a testament to her courage and honesty.

In the ensuing days at the university, our interactions took on a new dimension. Ava's presence in my life became more pronounced. She started spending more time with me, not just in the context of academics but in casual, everyday situations. Our conversations, once dominated by discussions of programming and algorithms, now meandered into personal territories—hopes, aspirations, and anecdotes from our lives.

This gradual shift was subtle but undeniable. I found myself looking forward to our interactions, anticipating the comfort and ease that had developed between us. Ava, in her own unassuming way, was becoming a significant part of my daily routine.

Our lunches together in the university cafeteria were filled with laughter and shared stories. She had a way of making even the most mundane topics interesting and engaging. Her vibrancy and zest for life were infectious, and I often caught myself smiling at her anecdotes or marveling at her perspectives on various subjects.

Outside of the university, we began exploring the city together. These outings were a blend of adventure and discovery—from visiting hidden gems in the city that Ava adored to trying out new cuisines at quaint restaurants. New York, a city I thought I knew, unfolded new layers in Ava's company. Her enthusiasm and curiosity made each experience more vibrant and memorable.

As we spent more time together, I noticed the subtle ways in which we were growing closer. There was a comfort in Ava's company, a sense of ease that I hadn't felt with others. Her laughter, her playful jibes, her insightful comments—all these became familiar and welcome parts of my days.

Despite this growing closeness, the confusion within me remained. Ava had made her feelings clear, and in her typical fashion, had given me the space to process and decide. But the decision was not an easy one. On one hand, there was Ava—bright, beautiful, and sincere, offering a relationship that promised depth and connection. On the other hand were my plans, my goals, and the life I had envisioned for myself—one that, until now, did not include a romantic partner.

The complexity of my emotions was compounded by the realization that Ava's presence in my life had become something I valued deeply. Her friendship, her intellect, her spirit—all these had enriched my life in ways I hadn't anticipated. And now, with the possibility of something more on the horizon, I was left to ponder the implications of taking a step beyond the boundaries of friendship.

As I navigated my way through classes and coding sessions, Ava's gentle presence was a constant. She never pressured me for an answer, never made me feel rushed or cornered. This patience, this understanding of my need for time and space, only added to the respect I had for her.

The days turned into weeks, and our connection continued to deepen. The moments we shared, the conversations we had, all seemed to be subtly weaving a bond that was both beautiful and complicated. I was standing at a crossroads, with each path leading to a vastly different future. And as I pondered over my next steps, I realized that no matter what decision I made, it would irrevocably change the course of my journey—a journey that, in the heart of New York, had taken an unexpected turn.

Despite the vast social and economic differences that marked our backgrounds, Ava and I found a harmony that transcended these divides. Our worlds, so different in their origins, seemed to converge in a beautiful symphony of understanding and respect. We connected on numerous levels, discussing everything from the latest technological advancements to the complexities of politics. Our debates were as intense as they were enlightening, each of us steadfast in our views—she, a Democrat, and I, a Republican. Yet, these differences only served to deepen our understanding and appreciation for each other.

As time passed, I came to a profound realization. The connection we shared, the ease with which we communicated, and the deep respect we held for each other's views and beliefs was, in its essence, a form of love. It was a love not just born out of mutual attraction but out of shared experiences and a profound understanding of one another. And it was this realization that became my answer to Ava's earlier confession. I decided to embrace this love, to accept the unexpected turn my life had taken. I was ready to build a future with Ava.

Our weekends were a testament to this growing bond. We spent countless hours in her apartment, talking through the night. Our conversations meandered through various topics—our aspirations, our fears, the complexities of our chosen fields, and the intricacies of the world around us. These nights were filled with laughter, deep discussions, and moments of silent understanding that spoke volumes.

Sometimes, we would venture out into the city, our city, which had been the backdrop of our story. The cold New York nights held a special charm for us. We would sit beneath the Brooklyn Bridge, cups of coffee warming our hands, gazing out at the city lights reflecting off the water. The bridge, a timeless symbol of connection and resilience, seemed to echo the journey of our relationship.

During these moments, wrapped in the serenity of the night, we planned our future. We envisioned a life together, intertwining our dreams and ambitions, acknowledging the challenges but also the immense possibilities that lay ahead. Ava's aspirations in technology, coupled with my own achievements and ambitions in programming and artificial intelligence, painted a future rich with potential.

Our differences, rather than driving us apart, became the cornerstone of our relationship. We learned from each other, our conversations broadening our horizons and deepening our understanding of the world. Ava's passion for social issues challenged me to view problems from different perspectives, while my pragmatic approach to solutions provided a grounding balance to her idealism.

In Ava, I found not just a partner, but a companion for life's journey—someone who shared my passion for learning, my curiosity about the world, and my ambition to make a mark. Our love was a blend of respect, admiration, and a deep emotional connection that transcended the usual boundaries of romance.

As we sat under the Brooklyn Bridge, the cold air carrying the sounds of the city to us, I realized how much New York had become a part of our story. The city, with its relentless energy and endless possibilities, was a reflection of our relationship—dynamic, challenging, and filled with potential.

In those quiet moments, with the night enveloping us, I felt a sense of peace and certainty about the path we had chosen. Together, Ava and I were ready to face whatever challenges and opportunities lay ahead. Our love was a testament to the power of understanding and connection—a bond strong enough to bridge any difference, resilient enough to weather any storm. And as we sat there, lost in our thoughts and dreams, I knew that together, we could build a future that was as bright and enduring as the city lights around us.

Moving in with Ava was a decision that marked a new chapter in our lives. We agreed that I would pay half the rent, a condition that symbolized our partnership and mutual respect. Living together, we created a world that was uniquely ours, filled with shared dreams, late-night conversations, and the comfort of each other's presence. It was, undoubtedly, the most beautiful time of my life.

Our time at New York University swiftly passed, and soon, the day of our graduation arrived. It was a day of mixed emotions. On one hand, there was the exhilaration of achieving a significant milestone, the culmination of years of hard work and dedication. On the other hand, there was a tinge of sadness. I had invited my uncle and aunt to the ceremony, hoping they would share in this momentous occasion. However, their health issues prevented them from attending, leaving a void that couldn't be filled.

Ava's family came to the graduation, their presence a warm reminder of the support and love she always had. Meeting them was an experience filled with anticipation and a bit of nervousness. Ava had told me much about her parents, their accomplishments, and the expectations they had of her. They were accompanied by Ava's younger sister and brother, adding to the familial atmosphere of the day.

Her parents were gracious and kind. They welcomed me with open arms, expressing their appreciation for my academic achievements and the support I had given Ava. The conversation flowed easily, punctuated by laughter and shared stories. It was evident that Ava had inherited her charm and warmth from her parents.

Despite the joy and celebration, a part of me couldn't help but feel a sense of loss. The absence of my own family was a stark contrast to the presence of Ava's. I imagined how proud my grandmother would have been to see me graduate. She had been my guiding light, a constant source of encouragement and love. Her absence was a silent ache in my heart, a reminder of the solitary path I had often walked.

After the ceremony, Ava's family invited me for coffee. It was a kind gesture, one that made me feel included and appreciated. As we sat in a quaint café, surrounded by the buzz of the city, I couldn't help but feel a deep sense of gratitude for the family that Ava had brought into my life. They were a testament to the love and support I had found in her.

However, the day took a bittersweet turn when Ava left with her family to celebrate further. The moment she walked away, a profound sense of solitude enveloped me. For the first time, I truly understood the depth of my attachment to her. Her absence left a void, a quiet space that was usually filled with her laughter, her insights, and her presence.

Walking through the streets of New York, now so familiar, I felt a pang of loneliness. The city, with its towering skyscrapers and endless energy, seemed to echo my sense of solitude. I realized then how much Ava had become a part of me, how her presence had transformed my experience of the city and my life.

As the evening set in, with the city lights casting a warm glow on the streets, I reflected on the journey that had brought us here. From our first meeting at the university to sharing a home, from academic partners to life partners, our story was a tapestry of shared experiences and growth.

In the quiet of the apartment that night, surrounded by our shared belongings and memories, I felt a profound sense of longing for Ava's return.

The decision for Ava to leave New York and spend time with her family in Miami was one laden with a complex mix of emotions for both of us. It represented a significant change in the life we had built together, a life filled with shared dreams and routines. Her family, longing for her presence and eager to integrate her into their life in Miami, had extended an invitation that was both generous and timely. They offered her an opportunity to intern at a prestigious IT company, a chance that aligned perfectly with her career aspirations.

Understanding the importance of family and the value of the opportunity before her, I supported Ava's decision wholeheartedly. She had been away from her family for a considerable time, and rekindling those bonds was essential. However, the thought of her leaving filled me with a sense of impending loneliness. Our apartment, once a sanctuary of our love and companionship, would feel empty without her.

The decision was not easy for Ava, either. New York was not just a backdrop to our academic achievements; it was the city where our love had blossomed and grown. It was here, amidst the bustling streets and towering skyscrapers, that we had woven a tapestry of memories and experiences. Leaving it behind, even temporarily, was a step laden with a mix of anticipation and sorrow.

As we navigated through this period of transition, we made a mutual agreement, a testament to the strength and understanding of our relationship. We decided that both of us would seek job opportunities in New York and Miami. Whichever city presented a better opportunity for one of us, the other would follow. This agreement was not just a practical solution to our situation; it was a reflection of our commitment to each other and our shared future.

The plan was a balancing act between our professional aspirations and our personal relationship. The prospect of living apart was daunting, but our bond was strong, fortified by mutual respect and deep understanding. We knew that no matter the distance, our connection would remain unbroken.

In the days leading up to Ava's departure, we spent every moment making memories. We revisited our favorite spots in New York, from the serene Brooklyn Bridge to the lively streets of Manhattan. Each place held a special meaning, a story of the times we had shared. We talked about our future, about the possibilities that lay ahead, and the challenges we might face.

When the day of her departure finally arrived, it was a moment filled with a poignant mix of sadness and hope. We promised each other to stay connected, to share the mundane and the extraordinary, and to keep the flame of our relationship burning bright.

As Ava left for Miami, I felt a part of me leave with her. The city, which had been a witness to our love story, seemed to echo my sense of loss. Yet, there was also a sense of hope, a belief in the strength of our relationship and the future we were building together.

In the weeks that followed, we kept our promise. Our calls and video chats were filled with updates, laughter, and plans for the future. We talked about our job searches, the new experiences we were having, and the things we missed about each other. The distance, while challenging, also brought a new dimension to our relationship. It taught us the value of communication, the importance of support, and the strength of trust.

As I continued my life in New York, the city that had been the backdrop of our love story, I held onto the hope and the plan we had made. Whether it was New York or Miami that would become our next home, I knew that as long as we were together, any place would be a haven of our love and dreams. Our mutual agreement was not just a testament to our understanding; it was a promise of a shared future, a future that we were both eager to embrace, no matter where it took us.

As Ava's father began utilizing his extensive network in the IT industry in Miami, the likelihood of her securing a promising job there grew stronger. His connections and influence in the field were undeniable assets, and it seemed increasingly probable that Ava would find her professional footing in Miami. On the other hand, my skills and abilities in IT had opened up a significant opportunity for me in New York. The competition between the two cities—Miami with its familial ties and potential job for Ava, and New York with its vibrant energy and professional prospects for me— was intense.

New York had always been my first love. The city, with its dynamic pulse and endless possibilities, had become a part of my identity. The thought of leaving it was daunting, yet the love I had for Ava made this a sacrifice I was willing to make. Our relationship had matured to a point where difficult decisions were made with a balanced view, prioritizing our mutual comfort and future over individual preferences.

However, the absence of Ava in my daily life in New York was palpable. I missed her deeply—her laughter, her insights, the comfort of her presence. To cope with her absence and to save more money for our future, I decided to move into a more affordable studio apartment in Astoria, Queens. Astoria, with its diverse community and relatively lower cost of living compared to other parts of New York, seemed like the ideal choice.

The apartment was modest but functional, a far cry from the life I had shared with Ava. It served as a physical reminder of the new phase of life I was navigating—one of independence, self-reliance, and anticipation for the future.

Weekends were the hardest. Without the distractions of work and the hustle of the city, the absence of Ava felt more pronounced. I found solace in visiting Brooklyn Bridge, a place that held special memories for both of us. Sitting there, gazing at the expanse of the city, I would reminisce about the moments we had shared—the laughter, the debates, the quiet moments of understanding.

The bridge, a symbol of connection and resilience, seemed to echo my current state—standing firm despite the challenges, bridging the gap between my present and our future together. The cool breeze off the East River, the rhythmic hum of the city, and the distant lights all brought back memories of the nights we had spent talking about our dreams and plans.

As I sat there, lost in thoughts, I often found myself looking at the moon, wondering if Ava was looking at it too from Miami. The moon, a constant in our ever-changing lives, felt like a silent companion in our journey. It was a comforting thought, a reminder that despite the physical distance between us, we were still connected, still a part of each other's lives.

During these moments of solitude, I realized the depth of our relationship. It was not just built on love but on a profound understanding and respect for each other's aspirations and challenges. Our ability to think about each other's ease and well-being, even when it meant personal sacrifices, was the cornerstone of our bond.

As the days passed, my resolve only grew stronger. Whether in New York or Miami, I knew that our future together was worth any sacrifice. The beauty of our relationship lay in our mutual respect, our shared dreams, and our unwavering support for each other.

So, as I sat beneath the Brooklyn Bridge, with the cityscape spread out before me, I held onto the hope and the plans we had made. The distance was just a temporary phase, a test of our commitment and love. And I knew that, in time, we would be reunited, ready to embark on the next chapter of our journey together, no matter where it took us.

Part 2

The onset of my illness began subtly, with symptoms I attributed to the changing weather—a fever and a persistent cough. Initially, I paid little heed to it, immersed as I was in my freelance work. My expertise in machine learning and artificial intelligence had carved a niche for me in the industry, and the projects I was handling were both lucrative and intellectually fulfilling. Alongside this, I was actively applying to various companies, hoping to find a position that aligned with my career aspirations.

However, as days passed, my condition didn't improve. The fever subsided with medication, but the cough lingered, stubborn and unyielding. It was accompanied by a growing sense of weakness that I found hard to shake off. Reluctantly, I visited a doctor, who prescribed some medicines. Although I got better, the cough persisted, turning into a constant companion that drained my energy and left me feeling irritable and exhausted.

This physical ailment began to take a toll not just on my health but on my relationship with Ava. Our daily conversations, once filled with laughter and plans for the future, became infrequent and strained. Ava, unaware of the severity of my condition, perceived my lack of communication as a sign of neglect. She began to feel that I was deliberately distancing myself, a thought that pained me.

The truth was far from it. The constant cough and the fatigue had made me a shadow of my usual self. The vibrancy and enthusiasm that marked my personality were replaced by a bitter weariness. I found it increasingly difficult to juggle my health issues with the demands of my freelance work. The workload, which I had once managed with ease, now felt like a herculean task. Every day was a struggle to maintain my professional commitments while battling the physical and mental exhaustion that engulfed me.

Ava's growing frustration only added to the stress. Her messages, once a source of joy and comfort, became a reminder of yet another area where I felt I was failing. Her anger and hurt, though stemming from a place of concern and love, felt like additional burdens on my already weighed-down shoulders.

Our conversations became sporadic and tense. Ava's attempts to understand my situation were met with my irritable and short responses, a stark contrast to the patient and caring exchanges we once had. The distance between us grew, not just physically but emotionally.

My deteriorating health and the resulting impact on our relationship left me feeling despondent. I began to question my ability to balance my personal and professional life. The dreams and plans Ava and I had made seemed to be slipping away, lost in a haze of illness and misunderstanding.

In my moments of solitude, as I tried to cope with the persistent cough and the unrelenting workload, I felt a profound sense of isolation. The studio apartment in Astoria, once a place of refuge and independence, now felt like a confinement. The walls seemed to echo my coughs and my frustrations, reminding me of the growing chasm in my relationship with Ava.

As days turned into weeks, the realization dawned on me that this situation was unsustainable. I needed to take control of my health and find a way to bridge the gap that had formed between Ava and me. It was clear that my physical condition was more than just a minor ailment and required serious attention.

In this challenging phase, the memories of the times spent with Ava under the Brooklyn Bridge, our plans, and our dreams, served as a beacon of hope. They reminded me of the love and connection we shared, a bond that had weathered many storms. It was this realization that spurred me into action, to seek proper medical care and to reopen the lines of communication with Ava, to rebuild the trust and understanding that had always been the foundation of our relationship.

In my increasingly solitary life in New York, my social interactions had dwindled significantly. My shy and reserved nature, coupled with my commitment to Ava and my professional endeavors, had left little room for a social circle. The only exception was my friend, Ethan, who had been a constant in my life. Ethan often visited me and stayed in touch over the phone, providing a much-needed connection to the world outside my immediate concerns.

Following the doctor's advice, I underwent a series of tests, hoping to uncover the cause of my persistent cough and general malaise. I returned to the doctor with the results, a sense of apprehension growing within me. The look of concern on the doctor's face as he reviewed the reports did little to ease my anxiety. He explained that while the tests were inconclusive, more investigations were necessary. He tried to reassure me, saying that sometimes initial tests could be misleading due to various factors, but his words did little to alleviate my worry.

As I navigated through this period of uncertainty regarding my health, the strain on my relationship with Ava continued to grow. I had always prided myself on being open and honest with her, so I told her about my visit to the doctor and the need for further tests. However, Ava's response was not what I had hoped for. She struggled to believe that my health issues were genuine, perceiving them instead as excuses for my recent withdrawal and lack of communication.

This misinterpretation by Ava added an additional layer of stress to my already burdened state. Her doubts hurt me deeply, as I had never given her any reason to question my honesty. The physical distance between us, coupled with our recent communication challenges, seemed to have created a gap filled with misunderstandings and unspoken frustrations.

On one hand, there was my health, an increasing concern that cast a shadow over my daily life. The uncertainty of not knowing what was wrong, compounded by the doctor's worried expression and talk of more tests, was unsettling. I tried to maintain a facade of confidence, but internally, I was grappling with the fear of a serious health issue.

On the other hand, there was Ava, the woman I loved and planned a future with, who now seemed distant and unconvinced by my situation. Her doubt gnawed at me, adding emotional turmoil to my physical discomfort. I found myself caught between the need to take care of my health and the desire to bridge the growing divide between us.

Ethan, during his visits, noticed the change in me. He saw the physical toll my health was taking, and the emotional distress caused by the situation with Ava. He became a sounding board for my worries, offering advice and support. Ethan encouraged me to focus on getting better and to try to communicate more effectively with Ava about what I was going through.

As the days passed, I awaited the results of the additional tests with a mixture of fear and hope. The solitude of my apartment in Astoria, once a haven, now felt more like a confinement, echoing with the uncertainty of my health and the complexities of my relationship with Ava. The city outside continued its relentless pace, indifferent to the personal storm I was weathering.

In this challenging phase of my life, I realized the importance of health, both physical and emotional. The need to address my medical issues became paramount, as did the need to mend the misunderstanding with Ava. It was a time that tested my resilience and the strength of my relationship, a time that required patience, communication, and above all, the courage to face whatever lay ahead.

The day I received my diagnosis felt like the ground beneath me had given way. The doctor's words echoed in my ears with a surreal quality. "Stage 4 lung cancer, with an expectancy of three months." It was a sentence that shattered my world into a million irreparable pieces. Everything around me seemed to blur into insignificance as I grappled with this devastating revelation.

Walking out of the doctor's office, I felt numb. The bustling streets of New York, which had always filled me with energy and aspiration, now seemed distant and unrelatable. My thoughts were in a whirlwind—thoughts of my career, which I had nurtured with such dedication; thoughts of Ava, the love of my life; and the future we had dreamed of together. All of it now seemed like a cruel joke, an unreachable mirage.

When I told Ethan about my diagnosis, his reaction was one of shock and disbelief. He insisted that I should tell Ava, that she had the right to know. But I couldn't bring myself to do it. The thought of Ava's reaction—the pain, the shock, the sense of helplessness—was too much to bear. I couldn't be the reason for her world to crumble.

I made the excruciating decision to keep my illness a secret from Ava. I knew that if she found out, she would abandon everything to be by my side. But what good would it do? To have her watch me deteriorate, to put her through the agony of my impending death? No, I couldn't do that to her. I wanted her to remember me as I was, not as I would be—a shadow of myself, consumed by illness.

In my heart, I yearned for her presence, for her comfort. But reason overpowered emotion. I resolved to push her away, to create an illusion of disinterest, to make her believe that I didn't want the relationship anymore. It was the hardest decision of my life, but in my mind, it was the most selfless one. Ava deserved a chance at happiness, a life unmarred by the tragedy of my illness.

As the days passed, I enacted my painful plan. I became distant, responding to Ava's messages sporadically and without affection. Each message sent, each call ignored, was a stab to my own heart. But I reminded myself that it was for her own good. I could sense her confusion and hurt in her replies, her messages laced with concern and a plea for an explanation. It pained me to know I was the cause of her distress, but I believed it was better than the alternative.

In the solitude of my small Astoria apartment, I faced my own battle. I began the treatment, a regimen that left me drained and hollow. Each session was a reminder of the inevitable, yet I clung to a sliver of hope—hope that maybe, just maybe, I could beat the odds, that I could have more than the three months the doctors had predicted.

I spent my days in a haze of medication and treatments, interspersed with moments of deep reflection. The dreams I had for my future, the plans Ava and I had made, now seemed like fragments of another life. I found myself revisiting our memories—the nights under the Brooklyn Bridge, our laughter-filled conversations, the plans we had excitedly made. These memories were both a comfort and a source of acute pain, knowing that they were all I would have left.

I had once envisioned surprising Ava with a visit to Miami, to see the joy on her face and to create new memories together. But now, that dream, too, had faded into the harsh reality of my situation. In my moments of solitude, I grappled with a myriad of emotions—anger, sorrow, regret, and, above all, an overwhelming love for Ava.

As I navigated this harrowing journey, Ethan remained my sole confidant. His visits were my only connection to the outside world, a world that I had once been an active part of. He respected my decision to keep Ava in the dark, though he struggled with the weight of the secret.

In the quiet of my apartment, as I faced the uncertainty of each new day, I clung to the belief that my decision to distance myself from Ava was the right one. It was an act of love, the most profound love I could offer—to shield her from the pain of my illness, to allow her to live a life full of possibilities, a life she deserved.

Each day was a battle, a balance between holding onto hope and preparing for the inevitable. But through it all, my love for Ava remained the one constant, a beacon in the darkness of my reality. And as I faced each day, I carried with me the memories of our love, a love that was as deep and enduring as the city that had brought us together.

The return to my apartment in Astoria marked a somber acceptance of my fate. The four walls that had once symbolized my independence now felt like the boundaries of a solitary confinement, where I awaited the inevitable end. My days were a blend of pain, medications, and a profound sense of loneliness, punctuated only by Ethan's calls.

Ethan, who had secured a job in Boston, was my only link to the outside world. His concern for me was evident in his regular calls, but as time went by, his new job responsibilities began to take precedence, and our conversations grew less frequent. I understood and accepted this shift; life had to go on for others, even as mine was grinding to a halt.

The hardest part of my days was dealing with the emotional turmoil. The decision to keep Ava in the dark about my condition and to push her away had been excruciating. Yet, in my mind, it was the only way to protect her from the pain of my eventual demise. I wanted her to remember me as I was, not as I would be—bedridden, suffering, a mere shadow of the man she loved.

Ava's frustration and hurt were evident in every message she sent, for a chance to mend whatever she thought had gone wrong. Her words tore at my heart, but I remained steadfast in my resolve. I believed that this was for the best.

Then, one day, Ava did something unexpected—she came to New York, hoping to confront me, to give our relationship one last chance. When I learned of her arrival, my heart leaped with a mixture of joy and dread. The thought of seeing her, of being able to hold her one last time, was overwhelmingly tempting. Yet, I knew I couldn't. I couldn't let her see me in my deteriorated state.

In a desperate bid to maintain the facade, I lied to her, telling her I was in Boston with Ethan. It was a blatant untruth, and Ava knew it. The realization that I had lied only added to her hurt, solidifying her belief that I no longer wanted her in my life. Her voice messages, filled with tears and a heart-wrenching goodbye, were the hardest thing I had ever had to listen to. I cried with her, mourning the loss of what could have been, mourning the love we had shared.

Ava left New York with a broken heart, feeling betrayed and abandoned. And that was the last I heard from her. She never called or texted again. As painful as it was, this was what I had wanted—for her to move on, to live a life free from the shadows of my illness. But the cost of this 'freedom' for her was a heavy burden on my soul.

In the silence of my apartment, I was haunted by thoughts of what might have been. I longed for her touch, her presence, her understanding. I imagined telling her everything—about the cancer, about my decision to push her away, about my undying love for her. But these were just fantasies, figments of my imagination that provided cold comfort.

The days passed in a blur of pain and introspection. I spent hours looking out of the window, watching life go on in the streets of Astoria, a stark contrast to the stagnation of my own existence. The city, which had once been a canvas for my dreams and ambitions, now seemed distant and unreachable.

As my health deteriorated, so did my connection to the world. The physical pain was often unbearable, but it was nothing compared to the agony of emotional isolation. I had chosen this path, a path of solitary suffering, believing it to be an act of love. But as the end drew nearer, I couldn't help but question my decision. Had I been right to keep Ava away, to deny her the chance to say goodbye, to be with me in my final moments?

The loneliness was suffocating, a constant reminder of the price I had paid for my decision. Ethan's voice, once a regular comfort, now felt like a distant echo, a reminder of a life that was slipping away. And Ava, my beloved Ava, was just a memory, a ghost of a future we would never have.

In the quiet of my apartment, surrounded by the remnants of a life half-lived, I waited for the end, clinging to the memories of happier times. Times when Ava and I dreamed under the stars, when we walked the streets of New York, hand in hand, full of plans and hope. Those memories were now my only solace, a bittersweet reminder of a love that had burned brightly but all too briefly.

As I lay there, struggling with each breath, I realized the true cost of my decision. In trying to protect Ava from pain, I had inflicted the greatest pain of all—the pain of abandonment and unexplained loss. And as I faced my final days, I did so with a heart full of love and a soul filled with regret, wondering if I had truly made the right choice.

The realization that my life was drawing to a close brought a clarity that was as painful as it was profound. The journey from overcoming poverty, forging a path in a field I loved, and finding love in Ava, to facing an untimely end, was a cruel twist of fate. I had reached a point where my aspirations, my dreams, and my love were just within reach, only to have them snatched away by an inexorable illness.

As the days passed, my health deteriorated steadily. The vibrancy and vitality that once defined me were replaced by a frailty that confined me to my apartment. My world, once as vast as the New York skyline, had shrunk to the four walls of my small Astoria home. The bustling streets, the lively cafes, and the serene parks of the city were now just memories, vivid in my mind but unreachable.

I found myself in a state of introspection, reflecting on the life I had lived and the future I would never see. There were moments of profound sadness, moments when the weight of my unfulfilled dreams lay heavy on my heart. The thought of not being able to build a life with Ava, to not see where my career could have taken me, and to leave behind the people I cared about was overwhelming.

Yet, in the midst of this despair, there was a strange sense of peace. Accepting my fate had brought a certain calmness to my mind. The denial and the desperation to hold on to life had given way to a resignation to the inevitable. This acceptance, however, did not come easily. It was the result of many sleepless nights, countless tears, and an inner turmoil that tested the very limits of my strength.

I spent my days mostly in solitude, save for the occasional visit from a nurse or a call from Ethan. These interactions were brief respites from the loneliness, yet they were also stark reminders of what I was leaving behind. Ethan, though far away in Boston, tried to provide support and comfort in whatever way he could. But there was only so much he could do from a distance.

As I looked out of my window, watching the seasons change in a city that never stopped moving, I felt like an observer on the sidelines of life. The laughter and chatter of people on the streets, the hustle of daily life, all seemed part of a world that I no longer belonged to.

My physical condition grew worse with each passing day. The simple tasks of daily living became Herculean efforts. My body, once strong and capable, was now a source of constant pain and weakness. Every breath was a struggle, every movement a battle against the fatigue that enveloped me.

In these final days, my thoughts often drifted to Ava. I wondered how she was, what she was doing, and if she ever thought of me. The decision to keep my illness a secret from her and to push her away haunted me. In my heart, I longed for her presence, for her voice, for the comfort of her touch.

But my mind held firm to the belief that this was for the best. She deserved a life full of joy and opportunities, not the shadow of grief that my death would bring.

As the doctor's predicted timeline drew closer, I faced each day with a mix of apprehension and readiness. I had made peace with my fate, but the thought of the end still filled me with a sense of uncertainty. What would it feel like? Would there be pain? Would there be nothingness? These questions lingered in my mind, unanswered.

In my quieter moments, I found solace in the memories of the life I had lived. The challenges I had overcome, the successes I had achieved, and the love I had experienced with Ava—these were the treasures I would carry with me. They were a testament to a life lived with passion and determination, a life that, though cut short, was rich with experiences.

As I lay in my bed, looking at the ceiling of my apartment, I realized that my journey was not just about the destination but about the path I had traveled. The love, the pain, the triumphs, and the losses—all were integral parts of my story, a story that was uniquely mine.

In those final days, as I waited for the inevitable, I held onto the love I felt for Ava, the pride in my achievements, and the gratitude for the moments of joy I had experienced. My life may have been shorter than I had hoped, but it was a life lived with purpose and love. And as I closed my eyes each night, I did so with a heart full of memories, a spirit that had known passion, and a soul that had loved deeply.

As the final days of my life approached, a profound sense of melancholy enveloped me. The savings that were once earmarked for a future with Ava and a wedding that was to symbolize the beginning of our shared life were now being depleted on medical care and the necessities of my solitary existence. The irony of the situation was not lost on me—the dreams and plans I had meticulously laid out were dissolving into the harsh reality of my impending demise.

Each day was a stark reminder of the fleeting nature of life. The world outside my window in Astoria continued its relentless pace—the bright lights, the bustling traffic, the laughter of couples, and the vibrancy of New York life played out like a movie to which I was a mere spectator. The sounds of the city, once a source of energy and inspiration, now felt like echoes from a life that was slipping away from my grasp.

I found myself spending hours just looking out of the window, watching the world go by. The sight of couples walking hand in hand, their laughter and easy banter, was a poignant reminder of what Ava and I had once shared. The realization that I would soon leave this all behind, that my presence in this world would soon be reduced to memories in the minds of a few, was a thought that filled me with an indescribable sadness.

The closer I got to the end, the more reflective I became. Thoughts about life after death, about what lay beyond the realm of human understanding, occupied my mind. I wondered about the mysteries of existence, the purpose of life, and the nature of the soul's journey. These existential questions, which I had once pondered in the context of philosophy and intellectual curiosity, now took on a deeply personal significance.

My apartment, once a symbol of my independence, now felt like a waiting room, a transitional space between life and whatever lay beyond. The walls, adorned with pictures and mementos of happier times, were a silent testament to the life I had lived—a life marked by triumphs and challenges, love and loss, joy and sorrow.

As my physical strength waned, so did my connection to the world. The simple acts of daily living became monumental tasks. My body, once strong and capable, was now a source of constant pain and weakness. The cough that had been the harbinger of my illness was now a constant companion, each bout leaving me more drained than before.

In those final days, my mind often wandered to Ava. I thought about the love we shared, the plans we made, and the dreams we had for our future. I wondered how she was coping, whether she had moved on, and if she ever thought of me. The decision to push her away, to spare her the pain of my illness, was a choice that haunted me in those lonely hours.

My heart ached with the longing to see her one last time, to hold her, to tell her everything—about my illness, my love for her, and my reasons for keeping her at a distance. But I knew that it was impossible, a dream that could never be realized.

As the end drew nearer, I faced it with a mixture of fear and acceptance. The fear of the unknown, of what lay beyond the veil of death, was tempered by the acceptance of my fate. I had come to terms with the reality that my time in this world was coming to an end.

In my last days, surrounded by the fading echoes of a life once lived, I held on to the memories of my journey. The struggles I had overcome, the achievements I had attained, and the love I had experienced with Ava were the legacies I would leave behind. And as I closed my eyes each night, I did so with a heart that had known true love, a spirit that had dared to dream, and a soul that was ready to embark on its final journey.

In the dwindling days of my life, a bittersweet realization settled upon me—my passing would leave little imprint on the world. There was a strange comfort in this thought. The only person who might deeply feel my absence was Ava, and I had carefully orchestrated our separation to shield her from the pain of my demise. This was my final act of love for her—to spare her the anguish of witnessing my decline and to leave her with memories untainted by the brutality of my illness.

My life, which once seemed like it was on the brink of blossoming, was now quietly withering away. The thought that my death would not cause a ripple in the lives of others was both a relief and a reflection of the solitary path I had walked. There were no family ties binding me, no children to mourn my loss, no colleagues to miss my presence. Even my relationship with Ava had been deliberately distanced to minimize the impact of my passing.

In the solitude of my apartment, I often found myself thinking about my mother. I wondered where she was, whether she ever thought of me, or if she even knew about my fate. My father, too, was a mystery—his presence in my life had been so fleeting that I had no memories of him. The possibility of having step-siblings or other family members out there was just speculation, parts of my life that remained unknown and unexplored.

The desire to see my mother one last time flickered in my heart. I longed to look into her eyes, to ask her the questions that had lingered in my mind for years, to understand why she left. But my deteriorating health made such a journey impossible. The distance to San Francisco was insurmountable, not just in miles but in the physical capability I had lost to my illness.

As the end neared, there was a part of me that clung to the hope of a miracle—a sudden reversal of my condition, a life-saving treatment emerging at the eleventh hour. It's a common thread of hope that binds those staring into the abyss of death—the yearning for more time, for a chance to rewrite the ending. But deep down, I knew that no such miracle awaited me. My journey was reaching its inevitable conclusion, and I had come to terms with that reality.

In my moments of reflection, I considered the life I had lived. There were regrets, of course—dreams unfulfilled, love left unexpressed, a future cut short. But there were also moments of triumph, of joy, of genuine connection. My time with Ava, though now tinged with sorrow, was a chapter in my life that I cherished deeply. The accomplishments in my career, my journey from poverty to success, were testaments to my determination and resilience.

As I lay in bed, each breath more labored than the last, I thought about the legacy we leave behind. For some, it's a tangible imprint—children, achievements, a marked impact on the world. For others, like me, it's a quieter legacy—a few lives touched, moments shared, a fleeting presence in the vast tapestry of life.

In my final days, I found a certain peace in accepting my fate. My life had been a solitary journey, marked by brief moments of connection and love. And as I prepared to leave this world, I did so with the knowledge that my departure would be as quiet as my existence had been. My story was one of many, a brief flicker in the endless cycle of life and death. And as the curtain fell on my time in this world, I closed my eyes, content in the knowledge that I had lived my truth, loved deeply, and left behind a small, but meaningful, imprint on the hearts I had touched.

As the dawn of what I sensed to be my last day broke, I awoke to a fit of coughing so severe it felt like every breath was a battle. The room around me, once a familiar space, now felt like a confining shell, each object a reminder of a life that was slipping away. I mustered the little strength I had left to get a bottle of water from the fridge, but my body betrayed me. My legs gave way, and I collapsed onto the cold floor, a stark reminder of my frailty.

Lying there, my vision blurred, I felt a strange sense of detachment. The pain and the struggle for air seemed distant, as if I was an onlooker to my own demise. The apartment, with its muted sounds and dim light, felt otherworldly, a transitional realm between life and death.

In those moments, a brilliant white light filled my vision. It was so bright, so overwhelming, that it washed away the contours of my apartment, leaving me in a sea of luminescence. I thought I saw figures entering the room, their forms indistinct in the glaring light. My mind, teetering on the edge of consciousness, conjured the thought that these were my angels of death, come to guide me to the beyond.

As they approached, I tried to discern their faces, to glean some recognition or understanding from their features. But the light was too intense, blurring their forms, making it impossible to see clearly. A sense of calm enveloped me, a surrender to the inevitable. I had always wondered what the final moments of life would be like, and now, here I was, experiencing the last threads of existence unraveling.

My breathing became more labored, each inhalation a Herculean effort. The figures seemed to hover over me, their presence both comforting and unnerving. In my heart, I wished for one last chance to see Ava, to tell her the truth, to express my undying love. But that was a wish destined to go unfulfilled.

The sounds of the world faded into a distant echo, the struggles of my body growing fainter. My thoughts drifted to my life—the highs and lows, the love and loss, the dreams and disappointments. It was a tapestry of experiences, woven with the threads of joy, pain, love, and sorrow.

As the end neared, a profound sense of peace washed over me. The struggles of the past months, the pain, the loneliness, and the heartache, seemed insignificant in the face of the vastness that awaited. I felt myself letting go, releasing the ties that bound me to the physical world.

In those final moments, as my breaths grew shallower, the figures in the light remained by my side, silent sentinels to my passing. The boundary between life and death blurred, and I felt myself slipping away, carried by the tide of an unknown but inevitable journey.

My eyes closed for the last time, the white light enveloping me in its embrace. The physical world, with all its joys and sorrows, receded into the background. And as my last breath left me, I surrendered to the mystery that lay beyond, leaving behind the world I knew, embarking on a journey into the unknown.

As the intense white light enveloped me, my mind was caught in a whirlwind of confusion and pain. Disoriented and weak, I struggled to make sense of my surroundings. Was this a hospital room bathed in the harsh glare of surgical lights, or had I crossed over into some ethereal realm beyond life?

The cold, unyielding floor of my apartment where I had collapsed seemed like a distant memory, yet the echoes of that moment lingered with aching clarity. I remembered the overwhelming coughing fit, the desperate gasp for air, the feeling of my body giving in. But what followed was a blank canvas, a void in my recollection that left me grappling for answers.

Now, as I lay under this blinding light, my body wracked with pain, I found myself at the crossroads of reality and the unknown. The pain felt all too real, a cruel reminder of my mortal affliction, but the surreal brightness of my surroundings sowed seeds of doubt. Was this the realm of the living, where my physical ailments still held dominion over me, or had I transitioned to a state beyond death, where the soul wanders in its final journey?

The possibility that I might still be in the land of the living, confined to a hospital bed and clinging to the last vestiges of life, seemed plausible. The sterility of the environment, the muffled sounds that reached my ears— they hinted at a clinical setting, a place where life hangs in the balance, tended to by unseen healers.

Yet, part of me wondered if this was what crossing over felt like—a transition marked by confusion and a lingering attachment to the physical pains of the life left behind. Was this light the proverbial tunnel that souls were said to traverse, a gateway between the world of the living and what lay beyond?

My attempts to move or speak were futile, my body unresponsive, as if it no longer heeded my commands. This helplessness added to the surreal quality of the experience, blurring the lines between the tangible world and the ethereal. The figures I thought I had seen entering the room were now just shadows in my mind, their purpose and identity shrouded in mystery.

In this limbo, memories of my life began to float to the surface of my consciousness. Images of Ava, of our time together, of the dreams we shared—they paraded before my mind's eye, imbued with a sense of longing and loss. The thought that I would never see her again and never have the chance to reveal the truth, was a source of deep sorrow.

As I lay there, suspended in a state of uncertainty, I felt a profound sense of isolation. The journey of my life, with its trials and triumphs, its loves and losses, seemed to be culminating in this ambiguous moment. The prospect of death, once a distant inevitability, now felt palpably close, yet its true nature remained just out of reach, hidden behind the veil of my current experience.

In those moments of semi-consciousness, I grappled with the reality of my situation. The longing for clarity, for an understanding of where I was—in the realm of the living or the domain of the departed—was overwhelming. Yet, as I drifted in and out of awareness, I realized that the answers I sought might remain elusive, shrouded in the mystery of existence and the enigma of what lies beyond.

As my eyes adjusted to the darkness, a flicker of recognition sparked within me. The surroundings gradually came into focus, revealing the familiar confines of my Astoria apartment. This realization brought with it a cascade of memories—the diagnosis of terminal cancer, the debilitating illness, the harrowing bouts of coughing, and the collapse. But something was amiss.

Surprisingly, the excruciating pain that had been my constant companion was absent. I moved tentatively, half-expecting the familiar agony to return, but it didn't. Instead, my body responded with an ease and freedom I hadn't felt in months. Perplexed, I rose from where I lay, my movements fluid and pain-free. It was a stark contrast to the weakened state I had been in, where even the slightest motion was a struggle.

Glancing out the window, I saw the quiet, dark streets of New York. The sparse traffic and the position of the moon in the sky suggested it was the dead of night, a time when the city took a brief respite from its relentless pace. A glance at the clock confirmed it was 2:54 AM. The world outside was still, peaceful, a stark contrast to the turmoil brewing within me.

I walked back to my bed, a myriad of thoughts racing through my mind. Just hours ago, I had been on the brink of death, my body ravaged by disease, each breath a battle. But now, here I was, feeling healthier and stronger than I had in a long time. Was this a dream? A hallucination? Or had something inexplicable occurred?

Driven by a need for validation, I pulled back the curtain again, letting the faint city lights filter into the room. No, this was no dream. The familiar sights of my neighborhood were unmistakably real. I turned on the light and approached the mirror, half-expecting to see the gaunt, sickly reflection I had become accustomed to. But the face staring back at me was different—healthier, with a hint of color in the cheeks that had been pallid for so long.

The transformation was bewildering. How could someone on the verge of death suddenly reclaim their health in this manner? Was it a miraculous recovery, a medical anomaly? Or had my mind, in its final moments, retreated into a fantasy, a coping mechanism against the inevitability of death?

Sitting on the edge of my bed, I attempted to piece together the events. The last thing I remembered clearly was the overwhelming pain, the struggle for air, and then a blinding light. Had I passed out? Had my mind, in its distressed state, conjured up an alternate reality to escape the suffering?

Yet, the physical changes were undeniable. I felt revitalized, a sensation that was both exhilarating and confusing. My logical mind grappled with the impossibility of the situation, while a part of me dared to hope for a second chance at life.

In the silence of my apartment, I contemplated the bizarre turn of events. Questions swirled in my mind, each without a satisfactory answer. Had my body undergone some spontaneous remission? Was this a temporary reprieve, a brief respite before the illness reclaimed its grip? Or had something truly miraculous occurred, defying the boundaries of medical science and understanding?

The night stretched on, and I found myself pacing the room, each step a testament to the newfound strength in my body. The sense of confusion was overwhelming, but it was intermingled with a burgeoning sense of wonder and gratitude. If this was indeed a second chance, it was a gift beyond measure, a rare opportunity to embrace life anew.

As dawn approached, with the first light of day beginning to seep through the curtains, I knew that the coming hours would be crucial. I would need to seek medical advice, to confirm whether this recovery was real or just a fleeting anomaly. The thought of reaching out to Ava also crossed my mind, but hesitation took hold. What would I say to her? How could I explain this inexplicable turn of events?

In those early morning hours, as the city awoke to a new day, I stood at the crossroads of uncertainty and hope. The possibility that I might have more time, more life to live, was a notion that filled me with a cautious optimism. And as I watched the sunrise over the New York skyline, I embraced the mystery of my situation, ready to face whatever the day, and life, had in store for me.

As I switched on my phone for the first time in what felt like an eternity, the realization of the time that had passed hit me with full force. It was November 15th—I had been disconnected from the world for nearly twenty days. The phone lit up with missed calls and messages, mainly from Ethan. His last few messages conveyed a deep concern that gradually morphed into resigned silence, undoubtedly assuming the worst when I didn't respond.

I needed to affirm my astonishing return to health, to prove to myself that I was truly alive and part of this world again. Stepping out of my apartment, I encountered an elderly man. Our exchange of smiles and morning greetings was mundane yet profoundly affirming. It was an interaction that confirmed my presence in the world, a small yet significant acknowledgment of my existence.

The fresh morning air felt invigorating as I stepped outside the building. The familiar streets of Astoria, bathed in the soft light of dawn, seemed to welcome me back. Everything around me felt new, imbued with a beauty and significance that I had never fully appreciated before. The trees, the distant sounds of the waking city, the very air I breathed—all felt like blessings.

As I walked, my mind raced with thoughts and emotions. The most overwhelming of these was the realization that I had a chance to restart my life, to live out the dreams and plans that had been so cruelly snatched away by my illness. The prospect of reuniting with Ava filled me with an indescribable joy. The thought of seeing her again, of being able to hold her, to share this miraculous turn of events, was exhilarating.

Life, which had once seemed so fleeting and fragile, now felt like an incredible gift—a second chance bestowed upon me under the most mysterious circumstances. I found myself cherishing every step, every breath, every heartbeat. The mundane had become miraculous, the everyday extraordinary.

The world around me was waking up, and with each step, I felt more alive. The streets of New York, which had been the backdrop of my life's greatest joys and sorrows, now seemed like a canvas of endless possibilities. The realization that I had been granted more time in this world was both humbling and empowering.

My walk turned into a reflective journey, a celebration of life itself. I thought about all the things I wanted to do, the places I wanted to see, the experiences I wanted to have. But more than anything, I thought about the people who mattered to me—about Ethan, who had been a constant friend through my darkest times, and about Ava, the love of my life, whom I had pushed away to spare her pain.

The decision to reconnect with Ava was not just a desire but a need that surged within me. I longed to explain everything to her—the illness, the painful choice to distance myself, and this inexplicable recovery. The prospect of reigniting our love, of building the future we had dreamed of together, filled me with a sense of purpose and hope.

As the sun climbed higher in the sky, casting its warm glow over the city, I felt a profound gratitude for each moment. The past weeks, lost in the shadows of death, had taught me the true value of life. Every moment was precious, every connection meaningful, every experience a treasure.

In that beautiful morning, as I walked the streets of New York, I made a silent vow to live fully, to love deeply, and to embrace the gift of life with open arms. The journey ahead was uncertain, filled with questions and mysteries. But one thing was clear—I had been given a rare and extraordinary second chance, and I was determined to make the most of it, starting with reuniting with Ava and mending the bridges I had burned.

This second chance at life was not just a continuation of my existence; it was a rebirth, an opportunity to rediscover the world and myself. And as I continued to walk, each step was a testament to my renewed spirit, a spirit that had once faced the abyss and now soared toward the promise of a new beginning.

As I sat in the cozy coffee spot that held so many memories with Ava, savoring the mocha that was her favorite, a profound sense of gratitude washed over me. The morning sun streamed through the windows, casting a warm glow over the bustling café. The aroma of freshly brewed coffee, the sound of the barista at work, and the chatter of patrons created a comforting backdrop. This moment, simple yet so full of life, was a stark contrast to the lonely confines of my apartment where I had battled with illness and the looming shadow of death.

The realization that I was experiencing what could only be described as a miraculous second chance at life filled me with an overwhelming sense of awe. For so long, my world had revolved around the pursuit of career goals, financial stability, and the material trappings that denote success. But now, as I sat there, healthy and alive against all odds, my perspective had shifted dramatically. The sheer joy of being able to walk, to breathe without pain, to witness the beauty of the world around me—these were blessings I had previously taken for granted.

Yet, as I sipped the coffee, my mind began to grapple with deeper questions. This unexpected recovery, this gift of renewed health, surely it wasn't without a purpose. The thought that there might be a greater reason behind my second chance at life was both exhilarating and daunting. What was expected of me now? What was the purpose that I needed to fulfill?

These questions swirled in my mind, creating a vortex of uncertainty and fear. I contemplated reaching out to Ava, to share with her this incredible turn of events. My heart yearned to reconnect, to explain the reasons behind my distant behavior, to reignite the love we had shared. But my hand hesitated as I reached for the phone. A nagging thought held me back—what if this miraculous recovery was a precursor to something more ominous? What if there was a price to pay or a dangerous twist awaiting?

The idea that my second chance at life could be tied to a darker fate was unsettling. It cast a shadow over the newfound joy and appreciation I felt. The possibility that there was more to my recovery than met the eye, that perhaps it was not just a simple twist of fate, filled me with a sense of foreboding.

As these thoughts consumed me, and the bustling café seemed to fade into the background. I found myself in a bubble of introspection, disconnected from the lively scene around me. The steaming cup of mocha in my hands, once a symbol of shared moments with Ava, now felt like a link to a past that was both cherished and painfully complex.

In this state of contemplation, I realized that my journey was far from over. This second chance was not just a continuation of life as I knew it, but a new chapter filled with unknowns. The decisions I made going forward, the paths I chose to take, would need to be guided by wisdom and a deep understanding of the gift I had been given.

As I wandered through the streets of New York, the miraculous recovery that I had experienced began to feel less like a stroke of fortune and more like a chapter from a science fiction novel. The logical, scientific part of my brain struggled to make sense of it. How could someone on the verge of death suddenly recover, with no trace of a terminal illness? The more I pondered over this inexplicable turn of events, the more I felt that there was an external force at play.

The memories of seeing unfamiliar faces outside my building and in the hospital started to come together, forming a narrative that seemed straight out of a clandestine operation. Were these people observers, keeping tabs on my condition? The thought that I might have been under surveillance was unsettling.

I began to construct a theory: what if my miraculous recovery was the result of an experimental treatment? It was possible that I had been unwittingly involved in a secretive medical trial. Maybe a private corporation or a government health lab had developed a groundbreaking cure for cancer and had chosen me as a test subject. The prospect of being a living, breathing success story of a secret medical breakthrough was both thrilling and terrifying.

This theory raised a multitude of questions. Why me? Was it mere chance, or was there something about my medical history that made me a suitable candidate for their experiment? And more importantly, if this was indeed the case, what did they want from me now?

The idea that my recovery could be a part of a larger, more sinister agenda was frightening. If a group had the means to cure terminal cancer, they wielded immense power. Power that could be used for benevolent purposes, or for more nefarious ends. Were they monitoring me to study the long-term effects of their treatment? Or was there a more ominous reason behind their interest in me?

Another unsettling possibility was that my recovery was not just about the cure. What if I had been altered in some way, made better, stronger, or different for a specific purpose? The notion that I could be a pawn in a larger scheme, perhaps as a part of some experimental program, was a disturbing thought.

I decided to be more observant of my surroundings, to look for signs of being watched or followed. As I retraced my steps, I noticed little anomalies—cars that seemed to linger a bit too long, strangers whose paths crossed mine a little too frequently. The feeling of being under a watchful eye grew stronger.

With each passing day, as my strength returned and my health stabilized, the need to uncover the truth behind my recovery became an obsession. I started taking different routes, paying attention to faces in the crowd, looking for recurring patterns. But the elusive watchers remained just out of reach, their presence felt but not confirmed.

The weight of this mystery began to take a toll on me. The joy of my newfound health was overshadowed by the anxiety of the unknown. The once vibrant streets of New York now felt like a labyrinth, with potential clues and watchers around every corner.

As I grappled with these thoughts, the realization dawned on me that my miraculous recovery had come at a price. The peace and normalcy I had longed for were replaced by a new kind of turmoil. I was caught in a web of intrigue and uncertainty, a pawn in a game whose rules and players were unknown.

In this new reality, every moment was tinged with suspicion and fear. But one thing was clear—I needed to find answers. I needed to understand the true nature of my recovery and the intentions of those who may have orchestrated it. This quest for truth, fraught with unknown dangers and hidden agendas, was now the central focus of my life. And as I ventured deeper into this mystery, I prepared myself for whatever lay ahead, determined to uncover the reality behind the miracle that had given me a second chance at life.

Walking through New York's vibrant streets, I reflected on the strange faces I thought I'd seen during my illness. Perhaps it was just my imagination, heightened by the stress and confusion of my condition.

While the mystery of my miraculous recovery lingered, I chose not to dwell on these unresolved questions.

The realization dawned that my life might still be in danger, and a sense of urgency took hold of me. The world believed I was dead—everyone who knew me. My absence from social media and my general aversion to it meant that there was no digital footprint that indicated otherwise. This anonymity, which I had always valued, now seemed like a double-edged sword.

Determined to stay off the radar, I knew my first step was to erase any ties to my previous identity. My apartment, which had been my sanctuary, now felt like a tether to a past that I needed to escape from. With a mix of apprehension and determination, I made my way back to my apartment.

As I approached the building, I scanned the area cautiously, looking for any signs of unusual activity or people who seemed out of place. Everything appeared normal, but I couldn't shake off the feeling of being watched. Once inside my apartment, I moved quickly, gathering essential items—a few clothes and the cash that represented my life savings. My heart raced as I realized the next step I had to take.

Standing in front of the stove, I held my identification documents in my hand. These papers were proof of my existence, my identity in the eyes of the world. With a deep breath, I set them alight, watching as the flames consumed them. It was a symbolic act, severing ties to my old life, and as the last embers flickered out, I felt a mix of liberation and loss.

I kept only my ID card, reasoning that it might be necessary for any unforeseen situations where identification was unavoidable. With my few belongings and the cash, I left the apartment for what I believed was the last time.

Stepping outside, I took one last careful look around. The street was quiet, with the usual hum of city life playing out around me. Yet, the normalcy of it all felt surreal, given the turmoil inside me. I walked briskly, trying not to attract any attention, my senses heightened to every sound and movement around me.

My destination was unclear, but I knew I needed to put distance between myself and my former life. The bus seemed like the best option—a way to blend in with the city's many faces and disappear into the anonymity it offered.

As I sat on the bus, the city passing by in a blur, my mind was a whirlwind of thoughts and emotions. I had effectively erased my past, stepped off the grid, and now, I was a ghost in the city that had been my home. The uncertainty of what lay ahead was daunting, but there was also an adrenaline-fueled thrill to it. I was charting a course into the unknown, leaving behind everything familiar.

In this new reality, every decision, every move had to be calculated and careful. I was aware that the path I was embarking on was fraught with risks and challenges. But I also knew that this was a necessary journey, one that I had to undertake to ensure my safety and to discover the truth behind my miraculous recovery and the mysterious circumstances that surrounded it.

As the bus journeyed through New York, I watched the city with a new perspective. It was no longer just a backdrop to my life; it was now a labyrinth in which I had to navigate my new existence. With each passing mile, I felt a growing resolve to uncover the secrets of my past and to carve out a new path for myself in this altered reality.

Embarking on this unforeseen journey, I was acutely aware that my first and foremost priority was to go into hiding, and the most logical first step in this plan was to leave New York City as swiftly as possible. The city, with its myriads of memories and connections to my former life, was no longer safe for me. I needed to vanish into a place where my existence wouldn't raise any eyebrows, where I could blend in without a trace.

I decided that my immediate destination would be Washington D.C. It was far enough from New York to sever any immediate ties, yet familiar enough to navigate. The bustling capital, with its own fast-paced life, seemed like an ideal location to disappear into anonymity.

As the bus made its way through the streets of New York, I formulated my plan. My first stop would be the Grand Central Terminal, the iconic train station known for its grandeur and the throngs of people it handled daily. Its vastness and the constant flow of commuters made it the perfect place to get lost in the crowd.

Upon arriving at Grand Central Terminal, I was immediately engulfed in the usual hustle and bustle of the station. The majestic architecture, with its expansive main concourse, beautifully painted celestial ceiling, and the constant hum of activity, provided a sense of normalcy amidst the chaos of my situation.

Navigating through the throngs of people, I made my way to the ticket counters. The train service from New York to Washington D.C. was frequent and reliable, with Amtrak's Northeast Regional and Acela Express services providing multiple options throughout the day. I opted for the Northeast Regional service—it was less conspicuous than the faster Acela and blended well with my need for discretion.

Purchasing a ticket was a straightforward process. I chose a departure time that allowed me to blend in with the regular flow of commuters—not too early to stand out, nor too late to attract unnecessary attention. With my ticket in hand, I found a quiet corner to gather my thoughts and wait.

As I sat there, the gravity of what I was doing began to sink in. I was leaving behind everything I knew—my home, my city, and the life I had built. The uncertainty of my future loomed large, but so did the determination to uncover the truth behind my mysterious recovery and to ensure my safety.

The train journey to Washington D.C. would take approximately three to four hours, time I intended to use to plan my next steps. I would need to find a place to stay, preferably somewhere lowkey and off the beaten path. The idea was to stay under the radar, to avoid any unnecessary interactions that could lead to recognition.

As the departure time drew near, I joined the stream of passengers heading toward the train platforms. I kept my demeanor calm, trying to look like just another traveler among the many. The anonymity of the crowd provided a sense of security, a cover for my clandestine escape.

Boarding the train, I chose a seat by the window, allowing me the chance to watch New York recede into the distance. As the train pulled out of the station, I felt a mix of apprehension and relief. I was leaving behind a life that was no longer safe, stepping into the unknown with a resolve to protect myself and unravel the mysteries that had brought me to this point.

The journey to Washington D.C. marked the beginning of a new chapter, one filled with uncertainties, but also possibilities. It was a path fraught with risks, but one I was determined to navigate to safeguard my newfound life and discover the reasons behind my second chance.

Upon arriving in Washington D.C., my immediate action was to book a train to San Jose. I had always been drawn to San Francisco, but I knew that if someone was tracking me, they might anticipate my heading there due to my known connections. So, in a move that felt like something out of a spy novel, I decided to travel across the country from the East Coast to the West Coast, ending in San Jose, a less predictable destination and to stay off the radar, I am opting to travel by train instead of by plane.

At Union Station in Washington D.C., bustling with travelers and echoing with the announcements of departures and arrivals, I secured a ticket for a long-haul train journey to San Jose. Opting for a train with sleeper berths seemed the most prudent choice for such an extensive trip. It would afford me some privacy and a chance to rest, both of which were crucial under these tense circumstances.

Settling into my berth, a compact but functional space with a bed and a window, I felt a sense of temporary relief. This small, private area was my refuge as the train embarked on its cross-country journey. I watched through the window as the familiar sights of Washington D.C. gradually disappeared, giving way to the unfolding landscapes of America.

The train's route took me through various states, each offering its unique scenery. Virginia's lush countryside and quaint towns passed by my window in the early hours of the journey. At night, the rhythmic sound of the train on the tracks and its gentle rocking motion provided a soothing counterpoint to my racing thoughts, which oscillated between the recent tumultuous events of my life and what lay ahead.

As morning broke, the train was cutting through the heartland of America. I saw the diverse landscapes of states like Kentucky, Missouri, and Kansas—a patchwork of farms, fields, and small communities that formed the backdrop of rural America.

Traversing through Colorado, I was greeted by the awe-inspiring sight of the Rocky Mountains, their majestic presence a stark contrast to the inner turmoil I was experiencing. The journey continued through the unique terrains of Utah and Nevada, including a fleeting glimpse of Las Vegas, a city that felt like a world unto itself.

As the train entered California, I felt a mix of anticipation and anxiety about reaching San Jose. The changing landscapes of California, from its deserts to its lush regions, mirrored the transitions I was going through. San Jose was uncharted territory for me, a place with no personal connections, but it marked the start of a new chapter in my life.

This train journey was more than a physical relocation; it symbolized my passage from a familiar life into the realm of the unknown. As I disembarked in San Jose, I knew that my real journey was just beginning. I was stepping into a future filled with uncertainties, but I was ready to face whatever challenges lay ahead, armed with a resolve to uncover the truth behind my miraculous recovery and the mysterious circumstances surrounding it.

Exhausted from the long journey and the emotional toll of the past few days, I made my way directly to a hotel upon arriving in San Jose. The fatigue had built up, not just from the physical travel but from the mental strain of my extraordinary circumstances. Checking into the hotel, I bypassed the usual pleasantries and headed straight to my room, craving rest more than anything.

In my room, I finally allowed myself the luxury of a deep, undisturbed sleep. It was a rest that I hadn't experienced in a long time, and it enveloped me completely. For those few hours, I was free from the worries and fears that had been my constant companions, lost in a peaceful oblivion that offered a temporary escape from my reality.

During my transit from New York to Washington D.C., I had made a crucial decision to throw away my cell phone and laptop. It was a drastic but necessary measure. In today's world, electronic devices are not just tools of convenience; they are also trackers, capable of revealing one's location and activities. I couldn't risk being traced through my mobile location or laptop IP address. The thought of someone tracking my movements was unsettling and could potentially jeopardize my safety.

Disposing of my devices was liberating in a way. It disconnected me from the digital world, a world where I had spent much of my time. As someone who enjoyed internet browsing and surfing, being without these devices felt strange. The internet had been a significant part of my life—a source of information, entertainment, and a way to stay connected with the world. Now, cut off from this digital realm, I felt a sense of isolation, but also a newfound sense of freedom.

The absence of electronic devices meant that I was no longer leaving a digital footprint. I was virtually untraceable, at least electronically. This gave me a sense of security, albeit a small one, in the grand scheme of things. It was one less thing to worry about in my current situation, where every caution counted.

Being off the grid also gave me time to reflect. Without the constant bombardment of information and the distraction of digital notifications, I could focus more on my immediate needs and plans. I had a lot to figure out—my next steps, how I would sustain myself without identification and with limited funds, and most importantly, how I would unravel the mystery behind my miraculous recovery and the reasons for my being targeted, if that was indeed the case.

In the quiet of the hotel room, with no electronic devices to distract me, I felt a sense of clarity. I was at a crossroads, with the freedom to decide my next move without the influence or noise of the outside world. It was a daunting yet empowering position to be in.

As I lay there, I realized that my journey was far from over. There were challenges ahead, and I needed to be strategic and careful. I had to stay under the radar, at least until I had a better understanding of my situation. For now, the priority was to lay low, gather my thoughts, and plan my next move carefully.

This new chapter of my life, while fraught with uncertainty, was also an opportunity to start afresh, to chart a new course. And as I drifted off to sleep, I embraced this chance, ready to face the days ahead with a cautious yet hopeful heart.

For the next couple of days in San Jose, I followed a simple routine, spending most of my time sleeping in my hotel room and stepping out only to eat at nearby establishments. My goal was to recuperate fully and gather my strength for the next phase of my plan. Staying in downtown provided a sense of anonymity, but I knew I needed to move somewhere even more inconspicuous to remain under the radar.

I decided on Tahoe City as my next destination. It was a small town, yet a popular tourist spot, which made it an ideal location for someone like me looking to blend in without drawing attention. The charm of a small town combined with the natural beauty of its surroundings appealed to my desire for a peaceful retreat while I worked out my next steps.

The journey to Tahoe City was a transition from the relatively urban environment of San Jose to the picturesque, serene setting of a town nestled near a lake. I arrived in the evening, the chill of November already setting in, a noticeable contrast to the climate I had left behind. The cold was biting, but it was a small price to pay for the security and solitude this place promised.

I checked into a modest hotel on the outskirts of town, near the beautiful Lake Tahoe. The hotel wasn't the epitome of luxury—it was somewhat rundown and lacked the cleanliness I was used to—but what it lacked in amenities, it made up for with its location and views. My room offered a breathtaking panorama of lush green forests and the serene lake. The scenery was a soothing balm to my frayed nerves, and it made the choice of staying in a cheaper establishment worth it.

The tranquility of Tahoe City was a stark contrast to the bustling streets of New York and the busy corridors of San Jose. Here, the pace of life was slower, the environment more intimate. The town, with its quaint shops, local eateries, and friendly residents, exuded a warmth that felt welcoming. The scenic beauty of the lake, coupled with the surrounding forests, was therapeutic. It was the perfect backdrop for introspection and planning.

As I settled into this new environment, my thoughts often wandered to the circumstances that had brought me here. My miraculous recovery, the need to go off the grid, the burning of my identification documents, and now living in a small town, almost in hiding—it all felt like a surreal twist in my life's narrative.

Despite the beauty and peace of Tahoe City, I couldn't shake off the feeling of being a fugitive, albeit one without a clear understanding of who or what I was fleeing from. The lack of electronic devices meant I was cut off from the world in many ways, which added to my sense of isolation. Yet, this disconnection also provided me with the clarity and focus I needed.

I spent my days exploring the town and its surroundings, always mindful of not drawing attention to myself. The crisp air by the lake, the tranquility of the forests, and the majesty of the Sierra Nevada range in the distance were constant reminders of the beauty and complexity of the world—a world I was still a part of, despite everything.

In the evenings, I would sit by my window, looking out at the stunning landscape and contemplating my next moves. I needed to unravel the mystery of my recovery, understand the reasons behind it, and figure out how to move forward. The challenge was immense, but for the first time since my illness, I felt a sense of purpose and determination.

Living in Tahoe City offered me the perfect blend of enjoyment and solitude. The beauty of the place was enriching, and the quietness allowed me to think without distractions. It was a temporary sanctuary, a place where I could gather my thoughts and plan my future, a future that was as uncertain as it was hopeful.

As I delved deeper into the potential implications of my situation in the tranquility of Tahoe City, a pressing realization dawned on me. The most alarming possibility was that I might be entangled in the machinations of an intelligence agency or a criminal organization, potentially aiming to exploit me for their gains. This thought spurred a sense of urgency in me—I needed a new identity, a fresh start under an assumed name to evade any entities that might be pursuing me.

However, the task of acquiring new identification and eventually a passport under a false name was fraught with challenges. The process was not only complicated and expensive but also laced with risks. With my funds dwindling day by day, the financial aspect of this plan was a significant concern. Yet, I was confident in my ability to generate revenue through my programming skills. The issue was that using any digital device could expose me, making me traceable and jeopardizing my safety.

In this dilemma, I decided that the local library would be a safe starting point. It offered access to the internet without the risk of using personal devices. The library, a place of knowledge and resources, seemed like the perfect setting to research and explore various options for acquiring a new identity and to formulate a detailed plan for my escape.

I made my way to the nearest library in Tahoe City, blending in with the locals and tourists. The library was a quiet, unassuming building, its shelves lined with books and its computers offering a gateway to the world beyond. Here, I could conduct my research discreetly, delving into the depths of the internet to explore the possibilities that lay ahead.

Sitting at a computer in a secluded corner, I began my search. I looked into various scenarios and options that could aid my escape. This included understanding the process of acquiring new identification documents, analyzing the risks involved, and identifying potential safe havens—countries with less stringent entry requirements and a lower profile, where I could potentially start anew.

The process was exhaustive and overwhelming. The more I delved into it, the more I realized the complexity of the situation. There were websites and forums that discussed the creation of new identities, but the legality and safety of these options were dubious. I also researched countries that were known for their relaxed immigration policies and lower profiles on the global stage. These countries could offer me the anonymity I desperately needed.

As I sifted through this information, my mind was a whirlwind of thoughts and calculations. Every option carried its own set of risks and implications. The decision I had to make was not just about evading potential pursuers; it was about starting over, leaving behind everything and everyone I knew, including Ava.

After hours of research, I left the library with a mind brimming with information but also clouded with uncertainty. The path ahead was not clear-cut. There were too many variables, too many risks. Yet, I knew that inaction was not an option. I had to make a move, to take a leap into the unknown for the sake of my safety and freedom.

As I walked back to my hotel, the serene beauty of Tahoe City seemed to be at odds with the turmoil inside me. The decision I was about to make would alter the course of my life forever. It was a daunting prospect, but one that I was prepared to face. With each step, I felt a growing resolve to forge a new path, to navigate the challenges ahead, and to find a way to start over, no matter how arduous the journey might be.

Part 3

The night in Tahoe City was colder than usual, and the weariness from my constant vigilance weighed heavily on me. Seeking respite, I retired to bed early, hoping for a few hours of undisturbed sleep. However, rest was elusive as my mind, still fraught with unanswered questions and fears, drifted into a dream that felt unnervingly real.

In this vivid dream, a man appeared. He was of middle age, with a clean-shaven face, dressed entirely in black. His demeanor was calm, yet there was an intensity in his eyes that suggested he was more than just a figment of my imagination. He addressed me by name, acknowledging my confusion and fears with an unsettling familiarity.

The man began to unravel the mysteries that had plagued me since my miraculous recovery. He revealed that my revival from terminal cancer was no accident or divine intervention. Instead, it was the result of an advanced technological experiment, one that involved the implantation of a nanochip in my brain.

This revelation sent a chill down my spine. According to the man, this nanochip was not just a medical device; it was a sophisticated piece of technology connected to a satellite and an AI system. This system, he explained, was capable of tracking not only my physical movements but also predicting my next steps with the help of Artificial General Intelligence (AGI) applications.

He elaborated that the chip was continuously transmitting data about my body—from my heart rate to my blood sugar levels. But the most alarming aspect was its ability to read my thoughts. Every thought, plan, or intention I had was being monitored and relayed to this AGI system. This invasive surveillance extended to the point where the system could intervene in my actions, preventing me from doing anything that might be deemed harmful to me or detrimental to the objectives of those behind this experiment.

The stranger in my dream cited an example that resonated with my reality, lending credibility to his claims. He referred to the moment in the coffee shop when I hesitated to call Ava. He suggested that it wasn't just cold feet or second thoughts that stopped me; it was the nanochip, intervening to prevent me from revealing my miraculous recovery. The idea that an external force had such control over my actions was horrifying.

Furthermore, he hinted at the sinister potential of this technology—the chip could not only prevent actions deemed unfavorable by its controllers but also compel actions against my will. This level of control extended to life-and-death decisions; the system could theoretically stop me from harming myself or, more disturbingly, force me into self-destructive actions if my existence became unnecessary or a liability to their objectives.

The man in my dream continued, his tone grave and foreboding. He explained that the chip was a groundbreaking convergence of biotechnology and artificial intelligence, a prototype of what could revolutionize human capabilities and surveillance.

In the depths of my dream, the man in black continued to impart crucial information, offering me a glimmer of hope in the midst of this technological nightmare. He revealed that while the implanted nanochip in my brain was sophisticated, it was not infallible. There were ways to circumvent its surveillance, albeit temporarily.

The first method he described involved managing the duration and diversity of my thoughts. He explained that the chip had a downtime of three minutes; if my thoughts on a single topic exceeded this duration, the chip would successfully translate and transmit these thoughts. Therefore, the key was to consciously limit any train of thought to under three minutes before deliberately shifting to something else. This constant mental redirection would disrupt the chip's ability to accurately relay my intentions.

The second method was even more intriguing. According to the man, the chip's functionality could be impeded by water. He advised that when water flowed over my head, it weakened the signals emitted by the chip, making it impossible for the system to read my thoughts. The shower, then, was not just a place for physical cleansing but a haven for unmonitored thinking. He cautioned, however, to keep these 'shower thoughts' under fifteen minutes. Prolonged periods of signal disruption could raise suspicions among those monitoring me.

Armed with this knowledge, I felt a sense of empowerment. Despite the advanced technology embedded within me, there were still chinks in its armor that I could exploit. The man's advice was clear—as soon as I awoke, I had to head straight to the shower to recall and process the details of this revealing dream, away from the prying eyes of the surveillance system.

As the dream progressed, I found myself rehearsing this strategy. I practiced shifting my thoughts every few minutes, training my mind to be agile and unpredictable. I envisioned myself standing under the shower, the water cascading over me, providing a shield under which I could think freely, if only for a short while.

Then, as all dreams do, it began to fade. The man in black's figure became hazy, and his voice a distant echo. The urgency of his message, however, lingered in my mind, a stark reminder of the bizarre reality I was living.

I awoke from the dream with a start, the early morning light filtering through the curtains. The vividness of the dream and the critical information it contained were fresh in my mind. I lay there for a moment, collecting my thoughts, careful to keep them brief and disjointed, just as the man had advised.

Then, as instructed, I made my way to the bathroom and turned on the shower.

As the warm water cascaded over my head, I felt a sense of relief wash over me. This was my safe space, my sanctuary from the invasive surveillance of the chip. I allowed myself to recall the dream in detail, remembering every word the man in black had said. His advice on how to outsmart the chip was my first real weapon in this asymmetrical battle.

Under the shower, I replayed his words: the importance of limiting my thoughts to under three minutes, and the significance of water in blocking the chip's signals. It was a lot to take in, but I understood that mastering this technique was imperative for my safety and to maintain some semblance of privacy and autonomy.

The man's revelation about the chip's accuracy being only 60% and its reliance on AGI for interpretation was particularly interesting. It meant that the system was not infallible and could be misled. This knowledge was empowering. It provided a sliver of hope that I could regain some control over my life and actions.

As I stood there, letting the water envelop me, I thought about the complexity of my situation. I was a living experiment, part of something much larger and more ominous than I had ever imagined. The implications were vast, not just for me but potentially for humanity. The existence of such technology, capable of such deep surveillance and control, was a profound ethical dilemma.

The dream had been a revelation, a guide on how to navigate this new reality. As I turned off the shower, I felt a renewed sense of purpose. I knew I had to be cautious, to constantly outthink the chip and whoever was controlling it. My actions had to be unpredictable, my thoughts guarded.

Stepping out of the bathroom, I felt a mix of apprehension and determination. The road ahead was fraught with challenges, but I was not without tools and strategies. The man in black, whether a figment of my subconscious or something more, had provided me with a starting point.

The day ahead in Tahoe City seemed different now. The picturesque views and serene environment were the same, but my perception had changed. I was no longer just a man enjoying the beauty of a lakeside town; I was a man on a mission, a man who needed to stay one step ahead of the technology within him.

As I dressed and prepared for the day, I resolved to keep my thoughts brief and scattered, to use the shower as my think tank, and to remain as unpredictable as possible. The journey to uncover the truth and regain my freedom was just beginning, and I was ready to face whatever lay ahead.

As night approached in Tahoe City, my mind was consumed with anticipation and apprehension. The prospect of meeting the mysterious man in my dreams again was both intriguing and frightening. The revelation that someone, or something, was monitoring and potentially controlling my thoughts was a notion I struggled to come to terms with. Yet, the man in my dream seemed to be my only source of answers in this bizarre situation. He promised more details, and I was desperate for any information that could shed light on what was happening to me.

The man's instruction to ensure a sound sleep was clear—I needed to be in a deep slumber for him to communicate with me through dreams. This necessity led me to make the decision to take sleeping pills, something I approached with reluctance. The idea of chemically inducing sleep to facilitate these mysterious dream encounters felt surreal, yet it seemed to be my only option.

As I prepared for bed, my mind was a whirlwind of thoughts. I practiced the mental discipline of keeping my thoughts scattered and brief, mindful of the chip's surveillance capabilities. The technique was challenging, requiring constant vigilance and effort. Every passing minute was a conscious battle to maintain control over my own mind.

Taking the tranquilizers, I lay in bed, waiting for sleep to envelop me. The room was quiet, with only the soft sound of the wind outside and the faint hum of the heater.

In this quietude, my thoughts drifted to the implications of my situation. The possibility that an AI was analyzing my every thought was unsettling, making even the sanctuary of my mind feel invaded. The stakes were high, and the need to master the ability to control and disguise my thoughts felt like a crucial survival skill in this unprecedented scenario.

I pondered over the man in my dreams—who was he? A benevolent informant trying to help me navigate this labyrinth of surveillance and control? Or was he another layer in this complex web, a creation of the AI designed to manipulate me further? These questions swirled in my head, adding layers of complexity to an already intricate situation.

Despite these racing thoughts, the tranquilizers began to take effect. My eyelids grew heavy, and the room started to blur into the shadows of the night. The pills were pulling me into a deep sleep, a state where I hoped to find the man and the answers he promised.

Lying there, on the cusp of sleep, I felt a mix of fear and curiosity. Tonight's dream had the potential to unravel more of this mystery, to provide insights into the identity of those behind the chip, their motives, and possibly, a way to counter this invasive technology.

The last conscious thought I had before succumbing to sleep was a reflection on the bizarre turn my life had taken. From battling a terminal illness to being thrust into a world of high-tech surveillance and clandestine dream meetings, it was a narrative that defied belief. Yet, it was my reality, and I had to navigate it as best as I could.

As sleep finally overtook me, I drifted off with a sense of determination. I was ready to face whatever revelations the night would bring, ready to learn, adapt, and fight for my autonomy and safety. The dream world awaited, and with it, hopefully, the answers I so desperately sought.

In my dream, the same man reappeared, his presence now somewhat familiar in this surreal dreamscape. This time, he revealed something even more astonishing—he was not from Earth but an alien from a planet named Steva, part of a system camouflaged from human detection.

He explained that Steva, along with two other planets, Astra and Conveta, formed a system called Tera, situated about 1500 light-years away from Earth. This system was shrouded in what Earth's scientists perceived as an interstellar cloud. However, in reality, this cloud was an artificial construct, a sophisticated camouflage created by the inhabitants of Tera to conceal themselves from human observation.

The reason behind this elaborate facade, he explained, was to observe and study Earth without interference or detection. The technology to create such a cloud was beyond anything I could comprehend. It was an advanced form of stealth technology, manipulating gases and particles in space to create a barrier that rendered their system invisible to Earth's telescopes and detection methods. This level of technological advancement was both fascinating and unsettling.

He elaborated on life in Tera, describing it as significantly more advanced than on Earth, not only technologically but also in terms of lifespan and civilization. The inhabitants of these planets, including his own, lived lives that spanned centuries, far exceeding human lifespans. Their society had evolved to a point where they had mastered technologies that humans could only dream of, including the ability to traverse vast cosmic distances and create artificial planetary cloaks.

The concept of planets hidden in plain sight, masked by artificial clouds in space, was mind-boggling. It challenged every understanding I had of the universe and our place in it. The man's revelation painted a picture of a cosmos teeming with life and civilizations far more advanced than ours, watching us from afar, hidden behind a veil of their own creation.

This encounter left me with more questions than answers. Why were they observing Earth? What interest did they have in our planet and its inhabitants? And most importantly, why reveal this information to me?

The dream felt intensely vivid, the man's words echoing in my mind with a clarity that transcended the usual haziness of dreams. As he spoke, the scene around us seemed to emphasize the vastness and mystery of the universe, a reminder of how little we know about the cosmos and the potential life it harbors.

As the dream progressed, I listened intently, trying to grasp the enormity of what I was being told. The idea that I was somehow caught in the middle of an interstellar observation by an alien civilization was overwhelming. Yet, in the context of my recent experiences, it added another layer of complexity to the already intricate puzzle of my situation.

The man's revelations about his home planet and its capabilities were a stark reminder of the endless possibilities that existed beyond our earthly realm. As the dream neared its end, I was left in awe, my mind racing with the implications of this encounter and the information he had shared. The notion that an advanced alien civilization had not only observed Earth but had interacted with me directly was a concept straight out of science fiction, yet it felt undeniably real within the dream.

The alien's presence in my dreams, his human-like appearance, and his ability to communicate complex ideas so clearly suggested a level of sophistication in their understanding of human psychology and physiology. It was as if they had studied us enough to interact in ways that we could comprehend.

As the dream began to fade, the man's final words resonated with a sense of urgency and importance. He implied that there was a reason behind their contact with me, something tied to the nanochip in my brain and the miraculous recovery I had experienced. The connection between this advanced alien civilization and the events that had unfolded in my life was still unclear, but it was evident that there was more to this than mere coincidence.

Waking up from the dream, I found myself in my hotel room, the first light of dawn creeping through the curtains. The details of the dream were vivid in my mind, leaving me in a state of bewilderment. The revelation of an alien involvement added an extraordinary dimension to my already complex situation.

Lying there, I tried to process the information. The existence of the Tera system and its inhabitants, their technological prowess, and their reasons for hiding from Earth raised numerous questions. Why had they chosen to reveal themselves to me in this manner? What was their interest in my situation, and how did the nanochip and its capabilities tie into their plans?

The man's advice on how to outsmart the chip's surveillance momentarily took a backseat as I grappled with these larger, more profound questions about my place in a universe that was suddenly much larger and more mysterious than I had ever imagined.

As I got out of bed, the weight of this revelation hung heavily on me. The day ahead in Tahoe City seemed inconsequential compared to the cosmic scale of what I had just learned. Yet, I knew I had to keep moving, to stay one step ahead of whoever or whatever was monitoring me, whether they were from Earth or from a planet hidden behind an artificial cloud in a distant galaxy.

Over the next few days in Tahoe City, I dedicated myself to the challenging practice of controlling my thoughts, as per the guidance of the man in black from my dream. Limiting each thought to under three minutes was a difficult exercise, akin to placing guards on my mind. It required constant vigilance and a level of mental discipline I had never exercised before. To facilitate deeper, unrestricted thinking, I took to bathing twice daily, using the time under the shower to think freely, away from the prying surveillance of the nanochip.

In the subsequent nights, the man in black, who identified himself as an alien, returned in my dreams to elaborate on the intricate details of his plan and the world he came from. He described the planetary system of Steva, Astra, and Conveta, likening them to different countries on Earth. These planets, he explained, were part of a highly advanced space-faring civilization. Due to their technological progress in space travel, inhabitants of these planets frequently visited each other, engaging in activities akin to international travel on Earth.

He painted a picture of a cosmopolitan interplanetary society where cross-planet marriages were common, and citizens of one planet would reside or vacation on another, much like how people on Earth travel to different countries. Their societal structure and interactions were remarkably similar to human civilizations, but they were centuries ahead in terms of technological advancement.

The alien explained that life on these planets began much earlier than on Earth, which accounted for their advanced stage of development. Their planets, while similar to Earth in terms of supporting life, had evolved differently due to their unique environmental and geological conditions. This early start in planetary development allowed them to achieve milestones in technology, science, and space exploration far beyond what humanity had achieved.

Their advancements were not limited to space travel. They had also made significant progress in areas such as medicine, energy, and artificial intelligence, surpassing Earth's technology by leaps and bounds. The concept of a civilization that had mastered interplanetary travel and communication was awe-inspiring, opening up possibilities I had never even considered.

As he divulged these details, the man in black's descriptions of his home planets and their societies were vivid and compelling. It was as if he were painting a picture of a world that was at once alien and familiar, advanced yet relatable. The idea that there existed in the universe a civilization that mirrored humanity in some ways but was far ahead in others was both fascinating and humbling.

Each night, as I awoke from these dreams, I was left pondering the vastness of the universe and the potential for life beyond our understanding. The revelations about Steva, Astra, and Conveta challenged my perception of our place in the cosmos. It was a stark reminder of how much there is to learn and discover beyond our planet.

As I continued my stay in Tahoe City, these dreams and the information they brought started to shape my understanding of the mysterious recovery I had experienced and the strange circumstances I found myself in. I was beginning to see my situation as part of a much larger and more complex tapestry, one that extended far beyond the confines of Earth and into the realms of interstellar civilizations. The knowledge that there could be entities out there, observing and possibly even interacting with us, was a thought that filled me with both wonder and unease.

The man in black, or the alien as he claimed to be, had opened a window to a reality I had never imagined. His revelations raised countless questions about the nature of these advanced civilizations, their intentions, and how my own experience fit into this broader cosmic narrative. The notion that Earth was just one of many inhabited worlds in the vast expanse of the universe was a humbling realization.

Every encounter with him in my dreams left me with a deeper understanding of the complexity and diversity of life in the cosmos. It also brought a sense of responsibility, a realization that my actions and thoughts, now monitored and influenced by this advanced technology, could have implications beyond my own life.

As I integrated these new insights into my worldview, I became more determined to uncover the truth about the nanochip implanted in me and the real intentions behind it. The knowledge that my thoughts were being monitored made every decision critical. I continued practicing the techniques he had taught me—limiting my thoughts and using the sanctuary of the shower for deeper contemplation.

In the subsequent nights, the man in black continued to visit me in my dreams, each time revealing more about the advanced civilization he belonged to and the profound knowledge they had acquired. He explained that their researchers had unraveled five of the greatest mysteries that still perplexed Earth's scientists. These included the composition of the universe, the origin of life, the essence of what made us human, the nature of consciousness, and the purpose of dreams.

One of the most intriguing revelations he shared was about dreams. According to him, dreams were not just a subconscious reflection of our thoughts and experiences but a sophisticated form of communication. He linked this to the theory of quantum physics, a concept familiar to me, but apparently understood and utilized in far more advanced ways by his civilization.

He explained that his people had a different name and understanding of quantum physics, but for the sake of communication, he simplified it to terms I could comprehend. They had harnessed the principles of quantum physics, not just for theoretical understanding but for practical applications, far beyond what humanity had achieved.

Their advancement in quantum computing, quantum machine learning, and Artificial General Intelligence (AGI) was light-years ahead of Earth's technology. These fields were integral to their society, allowing them to achieve breakthroughs in various aspects of life, from interstellar travel to complex problem-solving and beyond.

Quantum computing, as he described, was the backbone of their technological infrastructure. Unlike traditional computing based on binary codes, their quantum computing harnessed quantum bits or qubits, which allowed them to process vast amounts of information at speeds incomprehensible to the human mind. This quantum computing power was the key to their advancements in other fields, including AGI.

Their version of AGI had evolved beyond our current understanding of artificial intelligence. It wasn't just about creating machines that could learn and adapt but developing systems that could exhibit a level of consciousness and intuition, blurring the lines between artificial and natural intelligence.

The man in black also touched upon quantum machine learning, a field where they had made significant strides. By integrating the principles of quantum mechanics with machine learning algorithms, they had created systems capable of predictive analytics and decision-making with unparalleled accuracy and efficiency.

As he shared these insights, the enormity of their technological prowess became apparent. It was a civilization that had not only asked profound questions about the universe and existence but had also found answers through advanced science and technology.

His explanation about using quantum physics for communication, especially in dreams, was particularly fascinating. It suggested that they had found a way to manipulate the very fabric of reality to establish contact, transcending the physical limitations of space and time. This method of communication was how he was able to appear in my dreams, a concept that was both awe-inspiring and unsettling.

Each revelation brought a mix of amazement and apprehension. The knowledge that such advanced beings were observing and possibly influencing my life raised countless questions about their intentions and the role I was playing in their plans.

As the dream sessions continued, I found myself eagerly awaiting each encounter, yearning for more knowledge and understanding. The man in black had become my mentor, guiding me through the complexities of a reality far beyond my previous comprehension. His teachings were not just about the advanced technology and science of his world but also about the broader implications of such knowledge.

He emphasized that their mastery of quantum physics and its applications was a testament to their civilization's pursuit of understanding the fundamental truths of the universe. This quest for knowledge was driven by a desire to explore the limits of existence, to unravel the mysteries that have long captivated sentient beings across the cosmos.

In these dream encounters, he often spoke of the responsibility that came with such advanced knowledge. Their civilization viewed this understanding as a tool for the betterment of their society, a way to enhance the quality of life and ensure the sustainability of their existence across planets. It was a philosophy that combined scientific advancement with ethical considerations, a balance they had strived to maintain.

His explanations about the quantum nature of dreams and their use as a communication medium were particularly thought-provoking. It suggested that dreams could be more than just random neural firings or subconscious processing, a gateway to deeper, more profound levels of communication and understanding.

The concept of utilizing quantum principles to establish connections across vast distances, even between different worlds, was a clear demonstration of how advanced their technology was. It was a form of communication that transcended physical boundaries, enabling interactions that were once thought impossible.

As I absorbed this information, the realization of the vast gap between our civilizations became increasingly clear. We were just scratching the surface of understanding quantum mechanics and its potential applications, while they had not only unraveled its mysteries but were also utilizing it in ways that were almost magical to us.

The man in black, in his subsequent visits to my dreams, began to unveil the more intricate sociopolitical dynamics of the Tera system—the collective name for the planets Steva, Astra, and Conveta. His revelations painted a picture of a complex interplanetary society, where advancements in technology and science were paralleled by struggles similar to those faced on Earth.

He explained that despite the impressive technological progress, these planets were not without their problems. Among the most pressing issues were sustainability and environmental concerns, significantly exacerbated by their advanced technologies.

The rivalry and cold war between these planets, much like the geopolitical tensions on Earth, had led to an arms race of sorts, but on a scale far beyond our nuclear capabilities. This competition extended to advancements in AI, quantum computing, and energy technologies, including sophisticated forms of nuclear power. While these technologies had propelled their societies to new heights, they had also brought about unintended consequences.

One of the most significant issues was climate change, a challenge that seemed universal across civilizations. The extensive use of advanced AI and quantum computing systems had led to a dramatic increase in heat pollution. Unlike traditional computing systems, quantum computers operated at incredibly high efficiencies but also generated immense heat. As these systems became more widespread and powerful, managing the heat they emitted became a significant challenge.

The man described how this heat pollution had altered weather patterns and impacted ecosystems on their planets. The pursuit of technological advancement had inadvertently led to environmental imbalances, disrupting natural cycles and habitats.

Moreover, their reliance on advanced forms of nuclear energy, while providing a vast and efficient energy source, had its own set of challenges. The waste produced from these nuclear reactions was highly potent and difficult to manage. While their technology allowed for safer handling and disposal compared to Earth's current capabilities, it was not without risks and environmental impact.

The alien detailed how these issues had led to a growing movement on the planets of Tera toward sustainability and environmental conservation. Much like Earth, there was a dawning realization that technological progress could not come at the expense of the planet's health. This movement was not just about implementing new technologies but involved a fundamental shift in how their societies viewed their relationship with their environment.

The man in black continued to reveal the harsh realities of life on Steva, Astra, and Conveta. His latest disclosure painted a bleak picture of the environmental crisis these advanced planets were facing, a consequence of unchecked technological advancement.

He described a world where the natural environment had been so severely impacted by pollution and heat from their technologies that the air outside had become lethal. The inhabitants of these planets could no longer live in the open air as they once did. The atmospheric conditions had deteriorated to such an extent that exposure to the outside environment for more than five minutes could be fatal.

As a solution to this dire situation, they had constructed what he referred to as 'linear and vertical cities' beneath vast mirrored facades. These cities were architectural marvels, stretching both horizontally and vertically, encapsulated under gigantic reflective surfaces that protected them from the harsh external environment. Within these enclosed cities, the temperature and environment were artificially controlled, creating a livable habitat, isolated from the polluted atmosphere outside.

The mirrored facades of these cities were not just protective barriers but also served to regulate the temperature within. They reflected the intense heat and harmful radiation back into space, maintaining a stable climate inside. This innovative approach to urban design was a testament to their technological ingenuity, but it also highlighted the severity of the environmental challenges they faced.

He explained that stepping outside these controlled environments required special protective gear and oxygen supplies. The residents wore advanced suits designed to shield them from the toxic air and extreme heat, along with oxygen masks to breathe in the polluted atmosphere. This protective gear was a necessity for survival outside the climate-controlled cities, a stark reminder of the planet's inhospitable conditions.

The man lamented the loss of their planet's natural beauty and diversity. He spoke of a time when they, like humans on Earth, could freely roam their planets, basking in the sun, breathing fresh air, and enjoying the natural landscapes. Those days, he said, were long gone. The cost of their technological progress was the loss of their ability to live harmoniously with their environment.

He described how their societies had once thrived in harmony with nature, enjoying the different weathers and the bounty of their planets. But as their technology advanced, particularly in areas like AI, quantum computing, and nuclear energy, they paid little heed to the environmental impact. The pursuit of progress and power overshadowed the need for sustainability, leading to the current crisis.

Their story was a cautionary tale about the consequences of prioritizing technological advancement without considering environmental sustainability. The mirrored cities, while a marvel of engineering and a testament to their ability to adapt, were also a symbol of what had been lost—the joy of living in a natural, unspoiled environment.

Environmental crises facing the planets of Astra, Steva, and Conveta, painted a picture of societies grappling with the consequences of their own technological advancements.

He described how Astra and Steva had managed to mitigate some of the worst environmental effects through the development of linear and vertical cities. These cities, architectural marvels under their vast mirrored facades, were a testament to careful planning and advanced engineering. They provided a controlled environment where life could continue in relative normalcy despite the hostile conditions outside. These structures stood as symbols of resilience, a solution borne out of necessity to shield the population from the devastating impacts of pollution and heat.

However, the situation on Conveta was markedly different and far more dire. According to the man, Conveta had failed to implement these protective measures in time. The planet, once teeming with life, had become a harsh landscape where survival was a daily struggle. The environmental degradation had reached a point of no return, making the planet's surface almost uninhabitable.

The population of Conveta had dwindled to a mere third of its former size, with only the wealthy and elite able to afford the luxury of artificial environments. These privileged few lived in isolated havens, shielded from the decaying world outside, while the majority of the population suffered and perished. The disparity between the rich and the ordinary citizens was stark, highlighting the social inequalities exacerbated by the environmental crisis.

The man explained that technology-wise, Astra was even more advanced than Steva. This advancement, however, did not equate to immunity from environmental challenges. Astra, despite its technological superiority, faced similar sustainability issues. Their advanced technologies, while remarkable, had come at a significant environmental cost. The linear and vertical cities of Astra, though more sophisticated than those of Steva, were still a response to a global crisis that had forced them to rethink their relationship with their planet.

As he spoke of these realities, the parallels to Earth's own environmental challenges were clear. The story of these planets served as a stark reminder of the delicate balance between technological progress and ecological preservation. It was a cautionary tale of how even the most advanced civilizations could falter if they neglected the health of their planet.

The plight of Conveta was particularly poignant, a grim example of what could happen when environmental warning signs are ignored. It underscored the importance of timely action and the need for sustainable practices to ensure the longevity of a civilization.

Planets of the Tera system focused on the grim reality faced by their inhabitants. The most tragic tale was that of Conveta, a planet that had once thrived with life and technology but now stood on the brink of collapse.

The inhabitants of Conveta, he explained, had reached a point of desperation. The environmental crisis had forced them to abandon most of their technology, effectively sending them back to a primitive state akin to Earth's Stone Age. The few machines, still operational, were reserved for the elite, exacerbating the divide between the privileged and the general population. For the majority, life had become a bleak wait for the inevitable end, with little hope of survival.

The situation on Steva and Astra, while currently more controlled, was heading toward a similar fate. The linear and vertical cities, despite being marvels of engineering and a temporary refuge from the environmental havoc, were not a sustainable solution. The man made it clear that these structures, for all their technological advancement, were still dependent on the planet's dwindling resources.

He painted a picture of a civilization in decline, where the very advancements that had propelled them to new heights were now leading to their downfall. The linear and vertical cities, once symbols of progress, were now reminders of the consequences of unchecked development. The resources required to maintain these artificial environments were being depleted at an alarming rate, and the ecological damage inflicted on their planets was irreversible.

The artificial environments, while providing temporary relief from the hostile outside conditions, were not self-sustaining. The energy demands to keep these cities habitable, to control temperature, air quality, and provide artificial light, were immense. As resources became scarce, it was becoming increasingly difficult to maintain these havens.

The man's description of life on these planets was a stark warning of the perils of environmental neglect. The inhabitants of Steva and Astra, despite their advanced technology, were facing a future where their planets would no longer be able to support life. The reliance on protective suits and oxygen to venture outside was a testament to the severity of their planets' degradation.

His narrative underscored the universality of the struggle for environmental sustainability. It was a tale of advanced civilizations grappling with the consequences of their actions, a scenario eerily reminiscent of the environmental challenges on Earth. The story of the Tera system served as a cautionary tale, highlighting the need for sustainable practices and a harmonious coexistence with our environment.

The revelations from the man in black took a darker turn as he delved into the plans of the Tera system's inhabitants regarding Earth. He spoke of their longstanding surveillance of human activities, monitoring Earth's evolution and environmental changes closely. Their interest in Earth was not just observational; it was born out of a dire necessity for survival.

According to him, the inhabitants of the Tera system, particularly those from Steva and Astra, had recognized Earth as a potential haven, a planet where they could migrate due to its relatively healthy environment compared to their dying worlds. However, their plan for migration was disturbingly catastrophic for humanity. He revealed that one of their considered options was to exterminate the human population to make Earth their new home.

The technological hurdle of reaching Earth, despite their advanced capabilities, was a significant challenge. Their spacecraft, even with the most sophisticated technology, had not yet achieved the ability to traverse the vast interstellar distances to Earth. This challenge was a primary obstacle in their plan of migration.

Moreover, the idea of annihilating the human race to occupy Earth had sparked intense ethical debates among the inhabitants of the Tera system. The morality of such an action was a contentious issue, dividing their societies. The prospect of committing genocide on a planetary scale to save themselves was a decision fraught with profound ethical implications.

The geopolitical dynamics between Steva and Astra further complicated this scenario. Both planets, despite facing similar environmental crises, harbored ambitions to independently occupy Earth. This rivalry had led to covert agreements and strategies, as each sought to ensure that they would be the ones to claim Earth for themselves.

The man in black described how this interplanetary geopolitical conflict was playing out. Both Steva and Astra were developing plans and contingencies to reach Earth first and establish dominance. The competition between these two advanced planets was akin to a high-stakes chess game, with Earth as the ultimate prize.

This scenario was unsettling to contemplate. The idea that Earth, with all its life and diversity, could be viewed as a mere refuge for alien civilizations at the cost of human existence was alarming. It posed a moral and existential dilemma of an unimaginable scale.

As I absorbed this information, a sense of foreboding enveloped me. The potential threat to Earth and humanity was a heavy burden to bear. The knowledge that there were beings out there, considering such drastic measures for their survival, was a chilling thought.

The revelation also offered a perspective on the fragility and preciousness of our planet. Earth, with its diverse ecosystems and rich life, was a jewel in the cosmos, attracting the attention of distant civilizations. It highlighted the importance of preserving and protecting our world, not just for ourselves but as a sanctuary in the vastness of space.

The man in black's narrative about the Tera system's inhabitants' plans for Earth took an intriguing scientific turn. He described their intention to not repeat the mistakes that led to their environmental crisis but to develop Earth sustainably post-occupation. However, the primary challenge they faced was the immense distance between their system and Earth, a hurdle that seemed insurmountable with conventional space travel technology.

The solution, he revealed, lay in the realm of theoretical physics, specifically in the concept of creating wormholes. Wormholes, as explained in the theory of relativity, are hypothetical passages through space-time that could create shortcuts for long journeys across the universe. These bridges, also known as Einstein-Rosen bridges, connect two separate points in space-time, theoretically allowing for travel between them at speeds faster than light.

He detailed how scientists from the Tera system were exploring this advanced concept. By creating wormholes at different points on Earth, they could potentially traverse the vast interstellar distances in a fraction of the time taken by conventional spacecraft. This groundbreaking method of travel was still in the theoretical stages on Earth, but for the Tera system, it was becoming a tangible reality.

Furthermore, he elaborated on another sophisticated concept from quantum physics they were utilizing: the theory of entanglement. Quantum entanglement is a phenomenon where pairs or groups of particles interact in such a way that the state of each particle cannot be described independently of the state of the others, even when the particles are separated by a large distance. This principle, he explained, was being used to synchronize time between Earth and the Tera system.

By applying the theory of entanglement, they could align the flow of time between the two locations. This meant that any individual traveling from the Tera system to Earth through these wormholes would experience time in the same way as on Earth. The synchronization of time was a crucial aspect of making their travel and potential occupation feasible.

As I listened to this explanation in my dream, the sheer scale of their technological capabilities was astounding. The application of such advanced theoretical concepts in practical ways was far beyond current human achievements in physics and space travel.

The idea of using wormholes for space travel, manipulating space-time itself, was a concept straight out of science fiction, yet here it was, being presented as a reality by an advanced civilization. Similarly, the use of quantum entanglement to control the flow of time was another reminder of the incredible scientific strides these beings had made.

This scenario, as narrated by the man in black, painted a picture of a civilization at the pinnacle of scientific advancement, capable of manipulating the fundamental laws of physics to achieve their goals. It was a civilization that saw Earth not just as a refuge but as a world to be developed sustainably, learning from their past mistakes.

The narrative of the man in black took another turn, revealing the clandestine activities of the inhabitants of Steva and Astra on Earth. He described how both planets, despite their rivalry and differing agendas, had established secret base camps on Earth. These bases were part of a broader strategy for their potential occupation of Earth, serving as outposts for data collection and planning.

The residents of Steva and Astra had been covertly visiting Earth for some time, blending in seamlessly with the human population due to their similar appearance. This ability to go undetected among humans was a significant advantage in their hidden operations. Their physical resemblance to humans was almost perfect, making it nearly impossible to distinguish them from Earth's inhabitants at a glance.

However, the man in black explained that despite their external similarities, the internal physiology of the Tera system's inhabitants was markedly different from humans. One of the most notable differences was their blood. The blood groups of the Steva and Astra inhabitants did not match any known human blood types. This distinction was a clear biological marker that set them apart, though it was not something that could be discerned without medical examination.

Additionally, he described how their internal organ structures were different in shape and function. While these variations were not externally visible, they represented significant deviations from human anatomy. These physiological differences were a result of their unique evolutionary paths and environmental adaptations on their respective planets.

The secrecy of their Earth operations was paramount, as neither Steva nor Astra wanted to alert the other to their presence or reveal their plans prematurely. This covert presence on Earth was part of a larger strategy in their interplanetary rivalry and ambition for Earth. Each planet was gathering critical information, assessing Earth's environment, resources, and the human population, in preparation for their eventual plans.

The man in black's revelations about these secret bases and the presence of aliens among us were startling. The idea that Earth was not just being observed from afar but was already a field of covert operations by alien civilizations was unsettling. It suggested a level of extraterrestrial involvement in Earth affairs far beyond what was commonly imagined.

The notion that inhabitants from another solar system were walking among us, indistinguishable from humans unless subjected to medical examination, was a concept straight out of science fiction. Yet, in the context of my extraordinary experiences and the information from the man in black, it took on a new level of credibility.

As I awoke from the dream, I pondered the implications of his words. The presence of these alien visitors raised numerous questions about their intentions, the extent of their infiltration, and what their ultimate plans for Earth might be. The knowledge of their hidden bases and activities was a revelation that challenged the perceived boundaries between Earth and the rest of the cosmos.

The man's narratives, unfolding night after night in my dreams, were painting a picture of a complex interstellar situation with Earth unwittingly at its center. It was a scenario that required careful consideration and a deeper understanding of the potential risks and implications for humanity. In my ongoing series of dreams, the man in black continued to unravel the complex narrative involving the Tera system and its interest in Earth. He revealed a startling aspect of their plan, which directly involved me. According to him, the inhabitants of Steva and Astra had utilized their advanced Artificial General Intelligence (AGI) systems to identify an individual on Earth who could be instrumental in executing their plans for planetary occupation. This system had singled me out based on various parameters, including my high IQ, efficiency in programming, and my recent battle with cancer.

He explained that my illness, which was considered terminal on Earth, was, in fact, easily curable with the advanced biotechnology available on Steva and Astra. Cancer, in their societies, was treated much like any common, curable disease on Earth. It was this aspect of my history that made me a prime candidate for their plan— someone who had faced death and understood the preciousness of life.

The man described how, unbeknownst to me, I was taken to one of their covert base camps on Earth during my illness. There, using their advanced medical technology, they cured my cancer. This act, which I had perceived as a miraculous recovery, was actually a calculated move by the inhabitants of the Tera system. It was a demonstration of their technological prowess and a means to gain leverage over me.

During this clandestine medical intervention, they implanted a nanochip in my brain. This chip was not just a tool for curing my illness; it was a device for them to exert control over me. The chip was connected to their AGI system, allowing them to monitor my thoughts, actions, and potentially manipulate my behavior to suit their agenda.

The revelation that my miraculous recovery from cancer was a strategic move by an alien civilization and not a natural occurrence was shocking. It reframed my entire experience and recovery in a new, more ominous light. The fact that they could cure such a disease with ease spoke volumes about their level of advancement in biotechnology.

The man in black's explanation highlighted the ethical complexities of their actions. While they had saved my life, it was not out of altruism but for their utilitarian purposes. The implantation of the microchip without my knowledge or consent was a violation of my autonomy, turning me into an unwitting pawn in their interstellar strategy.

As I processed this information, I grappled with the implications of being chosen by an advanced alien civilization as a key figure in their plans for Earth. The realization that I was being monitored and potentially controlled by an extraterrestrial intelligence was deeply unsettling.

The man in black's revelations painted a picture of a cosmic chess game, with Earth as the prize and me as an unwitting player. The complexity of this situation, involving advanced alien civilizations, interstellar politics, and cutting-edge technology, was overwhelming. As the sun rose over Tahoe City, I was left to ponder my role in this grand scheme and how I could navigate this extraordinary and unprecedented situation.

In the ongoing narrative of my dreams, the man in black revealed another crucial piece of the puzzle. He spoke of a man named Dr. Alexander Roth, a name that resonated with familiarity and significance. Dr. Roth was renowned as a brilliant entrepreneur and a visionary in the fields of AI, quantum mechanics, and space technology. His ambitious startups and groundbreaking ideas had positioned him at the forefront of technological innovation on Earth.

Dr. Roth, as described by the man in black, was more than just an entrepreneur; he was a catalyst for a global technological race. His ventures in AI, quantum computing, and space exploration had sparked a wave of similar startups worldwide, each striving to push the boundaries of these fields. His influence was such that his ideas and projects were shaping the future trajectory of technology and scientific exploration.

Among his various enterprises, Dr. Roth had established four distinct companies, each dedicated to advancing a specific area of technology. One focused on AI, developing algorithms and systems that were at the cutting edge of machine learning and artificial intelligence.

Another was immersed in quantum computing, working on harnessing the power of quantum mechanics to revolutionize data processing and computational capabilities.

The third company was a foray into space technology, exploring innovative approaches to space travel, satellite deployment, and extraterrestrial exploration. The fourth, and perhaps the most secretive, was a collaboration with government agencies, including the Pentagon, the Defense Advanced Research Projects Agency (DARPA), and NASA.

This particular project, as revealed by the man in black, was shrouded in secrecy. It was a joint venture between Dr. Roth's company and the government, funded by public sector resources but operating under a veil of confidentiality. The details of this collaboration were not publicly known, and the project was kept away from the media and public scrutiny.

The man in black hinted that Dr. Roth's involvement with these government agencies was more than just a business partnership. It was part of a larger, more complex agenda that tied into the plans of the Tera system's inhabitants. Dr. Roth's advancements in technology, particularly in areas that were key to interstellar travel and communication, had caught the attention of the inhabitants of Steva and Astra.

He suggested that Dr. Roth's work, especially his collaboration with the government, might be playing a pivotal role in the plans for Earth's occupation. The technological breakthroughs achieved by Dr. Roth's companies could potentially be harnessed or exploited by these alien civilizations for their purposes.

As I listened to this revelation in my dream, I realized the gravity of the situation. Dr. Roth, a figure celebrated for his genius and contributions to technological progress, might unknowingly be a central figure in an interstellar plot. His work, while groundbreaking, could be a double-edged sword, with implications far beyond what was intended.

Awakening from the dream, I was left to ponder the connections between Dr. Roth's technological pursuits and the covert plans of the Tera system's inhabitants. The intertwining of Earth's technological race with the hidden agendas of alien civilizations was a thought-provoking scenario. It raised questions about the unintended consequences of our technological advancements and the potential for these achievements to intersect with extraterrestrial interests. As the day broke, these revelations hung over me, a reminder of the intricate and potentially precarious relationship between Earth's technological progress and the broader cosmic environment.

The thought that our advancements in AI, quantum computing, and space exploration might align with or even facilitate the interests of advanced alien civilizations was both fascinating and alarming. It underscored the need for responsible innovation and heightened awareness of the broader implications of our scientific endeavors.

Dr. Roth's work, particularly his secretive project with government agencies, took on a new significance in light of this information. It posed the question of how much we truly understood about the impact and reach of our technological discoveries. The possibility that these breakthroughs could be of interest to, or even manipulated by, extraterrestrial beings was a stark reminder of the unknown variables in the equation of scientific progress.

The revelations about Dr. Roth and his enterprises, delivered through these mysterious dreams, painted a picture of a world where the line between human innovation and alien intervention was blurred. It was a world where our quest for knowledge and advancement might intersect with interstellar interests in ways we had yet to comprehend.

As I contemplated these thoughts, the serene morning in Tahoe City provided a stark contrast to the complex web of interstellar politics and cosmic strategies unraveling in my dreams. The role of individuals like Dr. Roth, and potentially myself, in this grand cosmic narrative was becoming increasingly evident. It was a narrative that spanned beyond our planet, encompassing the aspirations and survival of civilizations light-years away.

These dreams, whether a product of my subconscious or a genuine connection to an alien intelligence, had opened my eyes to a reality far more complex than I had ever imagined. They highlighted the interconnectedness of our universe and the potential for Earth's future to be influenced by forces beyond our current understanding. As the day unfolded, I carried with me a heightened sense of curiosity and caution, aware of the vast, uncharted territories we were venturing into with each scientific breakthrough.

In my dreams, the man in black continued to weave the intricate tapestry of interstellar intrigue, revealing a significant development involving Dr. Alexander Roth's secret project. He disclosed that Dr. Roth, a pioneer in AI, quantum mechanics, and space technology, had inadvertently uncovered a dormant wormhole created by the inhabitants of the Tera system—a wormhole they had forgotten to close.

This discovery by Dr. Roth was monumental. Wormholes, as theorized in physics, are cosmic bridges connecting two distant points in space-time, potentially allowing for instantaneous travel across vast interstellar distances. The existence of such a wormhole on Earth, a remnant of the Tera system's exploration, was a breakthrough of unprecedented proportions.

Dr. Roth and certain elements within the U. S. government, including the Pentagon and US Space Force, were aware of the wormhole's extraterrestrial origin. They understood that it was a gateway created by the advanced civilizations of Steva and Astra, part of their plans for Earth. This realization had led to a clandestine operation, with Dr. Roth at the helm, to study and experiment with the wormhole.

The implications of this discovery were enormous. It meant that humanity was on the verge of unlocking the secrets of interstellar travel, a feat that was previously in the realm of science fiction. Dr. Roth's project was not just about exploring this wormhole but also about understanding the technology behind it, which could potentially enable humans to travel to the Tera system.

However, this groundbreaking discovery posed a significant threat to the plans of the Tera system's inhabitants, particularly those from Astra. The man in black explained that the Astra inhabitants were now aware that their forgotten wormhole had been discovered and were deeply concerned. They feared that if humans managed to harness the power of the wormhole, it could expose their plans for Earth and, more alarmingly, allow humans to enter the Tera system, posing a threat to their civilizations.

The Astra inhabitants were now in a race against time to destroy the wormhole before Dr. Roth and his team could fully understand and possibly replicate its technology. They wanted to keep their presence and their plans for Earth a secret, fearing that any knowledge of their advanced technology and interstellar capabilities in human hands could jeopardize their objectives.

As the dream unfolded, I could sense the urgency in the man's voice. He portrayed a scenario where interstellar politics, and the future of Earth were hanging in a delicate balance. The discovery of the wormhole was a pivotal moment, one that could either lead to a new era of human exploration and understanding or become a catalyst for conflict between Earth and the inhabitants of the Tera system. As I reflected on these revelations, I realized the critical role that Dr. Roth and his secret project could play in the future of humanity and our place in the cosmos. The discovery of the wormhole was not just a scientific milestone; it was a turning point that could alter the course of human history and our interactions with extraterrestrial beings.

In the latest development of my dream saga, the man in black disclosed a new twist in the unfolding interstellar drama. He revealed that the Astra inhabitants planned to induct me into Dr. Alexander Roth's team, the very group working on the discovered wormhole. Their objective was clear: they intended to use my skills to destroy the wormhole, thereby safeguarding their secrets and plans for Earth.

The man warned that while the Astra team might lure me with promises of financial rewards and freedom from the control of the nanochip embedded in my brain, their intentions were far more sinister. He cautioned that once I completed the task assigned to me, they planned to force me to commit suicide using the chip's control over me. This revelation was chilling—it suggested that my life was merely a pawn in their larger scheme, and my safety was contingent on their whims.

He further explained that the U. S. government, US Space Force, and Dr. Roth were aware of the alien presence on Earth and their covert activities. However, they were oblivious to the full extent of the Tera inhabitants' intentions, particularly the planned destruction of human civilization. This lack of complete understanding presented a dangerous blind spot in the human response to the extraterrestrial threat.

The realization that alien agents from the Tera system had infiltrated various government positions was alarming. It highlighted their strategic approach to gathering intelligence on Earth and influencing events from within. The discovery of their presence began with an accidental finding—the unique blood group of one of the aliens, which did not match any known human blood type. When the individual in question vanished the following day, it raised suspicions.

This incident prompted covert operations by government agencies to screen for similar anomalies. They conducted secret blood tests in key government and private sector positions, searching for these mysterious beings. The tests were kept confidential to avoid public panic and to prevent the aliens from going deeper into hiding.

As a result of these screenings, more samples with the unique alien blood group were identified, confirming the suspicion that the Tera inhabitants were more deeply embedded in human society than previously thought. This revelation forced the aliens to retreat from key positions, but it was clear that they were still operating in the shadows, carefully orchestrating their plans.

The U. S. government's decision to keep this information secret and to conduct discreet investigations into the alien presence was a strategic move. By not publicizing these findings, they aimed to conduct their search for these extraterrestrial beings without alerting them or causing public hysteria.

The stakes were high, and the implications of these revelations were profound. The presence of advanced alien civilizations with intentions to occupy Earth, the discovery of a wormhole, and the covert operations to uncover the truth about these beings painted a scenario of unprecedented complexity.

He revealed more layers to the complex interstellar plot revolving around the Tera system's intentions for Earth. He explained that I had been specifically chosen to infiltrate Dr. Roth's project because my blood test confirmed I was human, and I was controllable through the nanochip implanted in my brain.

Implanting such a chip in a human was no trivial task. It required precise alignment with the individual's mind and a sophisticated machine learning model trained to adapt to their thoughts. This complexity made it impractical to use such a method on a large scale. They had studied the intricacies of my mind in great detail, which was why the man in black was able to communicate with me through dreams. He needed access to the intimate details of my mind's structure, which he had obtained by hacking into their documents.

The man in black revealed his true intentions. He was an inhabitant of the Tera system, one of those who opposed the plan to destroy Earth's civilization. He sought to save humanity from the impending doom planned by his people. He warned that if the Astra team used me to destroy Dr. Roth's project, it would be a precursor to their larger operation to annihilate human civilization.

He spoke of a massive wormhole being constructed by the Astra team, capable of transporting hundreds of thousands of individuals. This project was unknown even to the Steva team, highlighting the internal conflicts and secrets within the Tera system itself. The Steva inhabitants, he noted, did not currently plan to destroy human civilization, unlike their counterparts from Astra.

The man in black urged me to be cautious and patient. The Astra inhabitants were waiting for me to let my guard down following my miraculous recovery, but they were monitoring me continuously. He emphasized the need for vigilance and preparedness for their eventual contact.

Days turned into weeks in the picturesque town of Tahoe City, where I sought refuge and clarity. The serene beauty of the lake and the tranquility of the town provided a stark contrast to the tumultuous revelations and responsibilities that weighed heavily on my mind. I had grown accustomed to exercising control over my thoughts, a skill I had honed to protect myself from the invasive surveillance of the nanochip implanted by the Tera system's inhabitants.

I found solace in the simple pleasures of the town, engaging with the locals and immersing myself in the everyday rhythms of life by the lake. These interactions were a welcome distraction, a way to ground myself in the present and momentarily escape the complexities of my situation. I would often sit by the lake, watching the water gently ripple against the shore, finding a sense of peace amidst the turmoil.

In the privacy of my bathroom, under the cover of running water, I would cautiously reflect on the information relayed to me in my dreams. These moments were the only times I allowed myself to think deeply about the man in black's revelations and the impending contact from the Astra team. I knew they were monitoring me, but they were not aware that I was fully cognizant of their plans.

The day finally arrived when the Astra team made their move. I had been anticipating this moment, yet a wave of apprehension swept over me. Despite my preparedness, the reality of confronting an advanced alien civilization and their sinister agenda was daunting. The knowledge that they intended to use me as a pawn in their plan to sabotage Dr. Roth's project, and ultimately, to facilitate the destruction of human civilization, was a heavy burden.

Their approach was subtle, a testament to their understanding of human behavior and their desire to keep their plans concealed. I was wary, constantly reminding myself that any interaction with them was laced with deception and hidden motives. They were unaware that I knew their true intentions, and I intended to keep it that way, using it to my advantage.

As I interacted with the representatives of the Astra team, I was careful to mask my awareness of their plans. I played along with their narrative, all the while searching for opportunities to subvert their agenda. My role had become that of a double agent, ostensibly cooperating with them while secretly seeking ways to thwart their plans and protect humanity.

My worry was not just for my safety but for the fate of Earth. The stakes were higher than any personal concerns. The man in black's warnings and guidance were a constant reminder of the need to stay vigilant and strategic in my actions.

In the midst of this covert chess game, I found strength in the beauty and normalcy of Tahoe City. The town and its people, unknowingly caught in the shadow of an interstellar conflict, were a reminder of what was at risk—the simple, unassuming beauty of human life and our planet.

Each day, as I walked by the lake or interacted with the locals, I carried with me the weight of the knowledge that Earth's future might hinge on my actions. The responsibility to act wisely and decisively was paramount.

I knew that any misstep could have far-reaching consequences, not just for me but for the entire human race.

In my interactions with the Astra team, I maintained a façade of obliviousness, carefully gauging their words and actions. Every conversation, every exchange was a dance of deception, where I had to skillfully hide my foreknowledge of their intentions. I understood that they were experts in manipulation, likely skilled in reading human emotions and reactions. Thus, I was meticulous in my responses, ensuring that nothing in my demeanor betrayed my awareness of their true agenda.

Despite the external calm, there was an undercurrent of tension in each of these encounters. The Astra team's representatives were cordial and persuasive, presenting their project as an exciting opportunity, a chance to be a part of something groundbreaking. Yet, beneath their congeniality, I sensed an air of urgency, a drive to move their plans forward.

The situation was a complex balancing act. On one hand, I had to convincingly play the role they expected of me, while on the other, I was desperately looking for avenues to undermine their operation without revealing my hand. The man in black's revelations had given me a glimpse into their world, their technology, and their way of thinking, and I used this knowledge to navigate the treacherous waters of this covert operation.

As I spent my days in Tahoe City, the normalcy of life around me was a constant reminder of what was at stake. The laughter of children playing by the lake, the peaceful rhythm of daily life, and the natural beauty of the surroundings were all poignant reminders of the Earth's innocence and vulnerability in the face of such a concealed cosmic threat.

In the quiet moments by the lake, I often reflected on the enormity of the situation. I was an unwitting player in an interstellar conflict, a human caught in the crossfire of alien ambitions. The responsibility to act in the best interests of Earth and its inhabitants weighed heavily on me.

Yet, amidst this chaos, there was a determination within me to do whatever it took to protect our world.

Each night, as I lay in bed, the thoughts of the day would swirl in my mind, a mix of strategy, concern, and resolve. The coming days would be critical, and I was acutely aware that the actions I took could alter the course of this hidden war. The future of humanity, unbeknownst to the people around me, might very well depend on the choices I was about to make.

The day unfolded like any other in Tahoe City, the tranquil ambiance of the town belying the turmoil within me. It was amidst this deceptive calm that the anticipated encounter finally occurred. A stranger approached me abruptly, his movements swift and purposeful. He handed me a small cell phone and vanished almost as quickly as he had appeared, melting into the crowd and leaving no trace of his identity.

Barely had I time to process this mysterious exchange when the cell phone vibrated to life in my hand. The call, as I had expected, was from the Astra team. The voice on the other end was cold and clinical, confirming my worst fears. They openly admitted to curing my cancer, not as an act of mercy, but as part of a calculated bargain. They revealed the existence of the nanochip in my brain, a tool they had been using to monitor and control me.

Their confession was chillingly straightforward. They knew my every thought, every intention, thanks to the chip. They declared that they had complete control over me and demonstrated this by forcing me to kick a stone with my foot. The involuntary action, driven by their remote command, was both humiliating and excruciatingly painful.

It was a stark demonstration of their power over me and a clear message that resistance was futile.

The voice on the call was unyielding as they laid out their terms. If I complied with their demands, they promised substantial financial benefits and the removal of the nanochip. But this promise was overshadowed by a sinister threat—if I dared to disobey, they would use the chip to force me to commit suicide.

The reality of my situation was overwhelming. The nanochip, initially implanted under the guise of medical treatment, was now revealed to be a tool of coercion. I was not just a survivor of a terminal illness, but a puppet bound by invisible strings—strings pulled by an advanced alien civilization with their own agenda for Earth.

As the call ended, I was left holding the phone, a heavy sense of dread enveloping me. The Astra team's manipulation had stripped me of my autonomy, reducing me to a mere instrument in their plan. The pain in my foot was a constant reminder of their control and the danger of defying them.

In the solitude of my room, the enormity of the situation sank in. I was at the mercy of beings whose technological prowess far exceeded anything known to humanity. The promise of financial gain seemed hollow in the face of the loss of freedom and the threat to my life.

The Astra team's intentions were now clear. They had chosen me as a key player in their scheme to destroy Dr. Roth's project and, ultimately, to pave the way for their occupation of Earth. The cell phone in my hand was not just a communication device; it was a symbol of my entanglement in an interstellar conflict, a conflict that threatened the very existence of human civilization.

As I grappled with the reality of my situation, I knew that the decisions I made in the coming days would be crucial. The fate of humanity and my own life hung precariously in the balance. The knowledge that I was being watched and controlled was a constant source of anxiety, yet I also realized that this might be my only link to thwarting their plans. The Astra team, despite their technological superiority, were not infallible. They had underestimated my awareness of their intentions, and this oversight could be the key to outmaneuvering them.

The cell phone was my direct line to the Astra team, a crucial element in this high-stakes game of espionage and survival. I understood that I needed to tread carefully, to maintain the illusion of compliance while seeking ways to subvert their agenda. Every action, every decision had to be calculated to avoid arousing their suspicion.

As I sat alone, contemplating my next move, the weight of responsibility bore down on me. I was not just fighting for my own life but for the future of our planet. The Astra team's plan to conquer Earth and eradicate humanity was a threat that I couldn't ignore. I had to find a way to use my position to protect Earth, even if it meant risking everything.

The peaceful surroundings of Tahoe City seemed a world away from the cosmic battleground I had unwittingly become a part of. The stakes were higher than any personal concerns. I was acutely aware that the actions I took could alter the course of this hidden war.

The challenge was daunting, but I was resolved to do whatever it took to thwart the Astra team's plans. The man in black, despite being an alien, had shown empathy toward humanity, and his warnings had prepared me for this moment. It was a reminder that in this vast and complex universe, allegiances could transcend planetary origins.

As night fell over Tahoe City, I steeled myself for the task ahead. The cell phone was my link to the Astra team, a tool that I had to use wisely. In this battle of wits and wills, I was determined to be more than just a pawn. I was ready to fight, to outsmart my controllers, and to safeguard the future of humanity. The journey ahead was fraught with danger and uncertainty, but I was not going to back down. The fate of Earth depended on it.

In a state of orchestrated worry, I awaited the next contact from the Astra team, carefully projecting my anxiety in my thoughts to convince them of my compliance. Two days later, the cell phone rang again, setting into motion the next phase of their plan. The caller instructed me to go to a secluded spot east of the lake, where a dense forest provided cover.

Upon reaching the designated location, I was greeted by an unusual sight: three individuals in surgical masks, their identities obscured. The one who spoke had a distinct Russian accent, claiming they were Russians. He spun a tale about Dr. Alexander Roth, alleging that he was developing a dangerous weapon aimed at Russia. They presented themselves as defectors or agents working against this purported threat.

The Russian-accented man explained that the weapon was based on quantum machine learning and that my task was to insert a specific code into its software. This code, he assured me, was encrypted and would simply deactivate the weapon without causing any other harm. By doing so, I would be saving countless Russian lives.

The offer they laid out was tempting and strategically crafted. They promised me a safe haven, financial security, and even cosmetic surgery to alter my appearance, ensuring my escape to any country of my choosing. Most importantly, they vowed to remove the nanochip, granting me the freedom I yearned for.

Yet, amidst their persuasive pitch, I remained acutely aware of the deception at play. Their story about Dr. Roth developing a weapon against Russia seemed far-fetched and played conveniently into global geopolitical narratives. It was clear to me that they were from the Astra team, using fabricated identities and stories to manipulate me into carrying out their agenda.

Their offer to remove the nanochip was likely another lie, a false promise to secure my cooperation. I understood that complying with their demands could have unpredictable and possibly catastrophic consequences. Tampering with Dr. Roth's project, especially something as advanced and sensitive as quantum machine learning, was a risky endeavor. There was no telling what the real effects of inserting their code would be.

Despite the apparent risks, I knew I had to maintain the illusion of being swayed by their proposal. Showing any hint of suspicion or refusal could trigger a fatal response via the nanochip. I had to play along, at least for the moment, while I sought a way to counter their plans.

As the meeting with the disguised Astra team members concluded, they unfolded the next steps of their elaborate plan. They intended to insert me into Dr. Alexander Roth's team, exploiting a vacancy for a quantum machine learning programmer. This role, due to its specialized nature, had been challenging to fill, providing a perfect entry point for their scheme.

The team handed me a laptop loaded with learning materials to prepare for the job interview. It contained a comprehensive set of programming tutorials, interview questions, and other relevant resources. Additionally, they provided me with a meticulously crafted CV, tailored to make me an ideal candidate for the position. This document was designed to pass any rigorous scrutiny that Dr. Roth's team might undertake.

To further solidify my cover story, they had altered my medical records to indicate a history of Stage 1 cancer, from which I had recovered. This detail was intended to explain any gaps in my employment history and add depth to my fabricated background.

The Astra team had orchestrated everything down to the finest detail. They provided me with an airplane ticket from San Jose to New York and assured me that my apartment in New York, which they had been paying the rent for, was ready for my return. Once settled in New York, I was to apply for the job using the link they provided. The CV they created was so compelling that they were confident Dr. Roth's team would promptly contact me for an interview.

Part 4

As the meeting ended, I made my way back to the hotel to pack my belongings for the journey to New York. New York was a city that held many memories for me, especially those of Ava. As I thought about returning, a flood of emotions and memories of Ava engulfed me. Our time together, the moments we shared, and the life we had envisioned in the city came rushing back.

I was painfully aware that my thoughts were being monitored through the nanochip. Every memory, every emotion I felt about Ava, was being observed by the Astra team. I struggled to control these thoughts, knowing the importance of maintaining a facade of compliance. However, the surge of emotions was overwhelming, a reminder of the life and love I once had and the stark reality of my current predicament.

As I packed my suitcase, the weight of the situation bore down on me. I was about to embark on a mission fraught with danger, deceit, and uncertainty. The plan to infiltrate Dr. Roth's team, to insert a code that could potentially sabotage a project of unknown scale and implications, was a daunting task. The promise of financial rewards and freedom seemed hollow against the backdrop of the enormous risks involved.

The journey to New York was not just a physical relocation but a step into a new chapter of this complex saga. As I left Tahoe City, I carried with me a mix of apprehension and determination. I was playing a crucial role in a plot that spanned beyond Earth, involving alien civilizations with agendas that threatened human existence.

Arriving in New York, the city's familiar sights and sounds brought a sense of nostalgia mixed with a sense of purpose.

I knew that the days ahead would be critical. The task of securing a position within Dr. Roth's team, under the watchful eyes of the Astra team, was a delicate operation. Every move I made needed to be calculated and precise.

As I walked the streets of New York, memories of my time with Ava haunted me. The city was a tapestry of our shared moments, each street corner and café evoking a sense of loss and longing. These memories were a stark reminder of the life I once had, now overshadowed by the extraordinary circumstances I found myself in.

Despite the emotional turmoil, I focused on the task at hand. The laptop provided by the Astra team contained all the information and tools I needed to convincingly apply for the position at Dr. Roth's company. I spent hours studying the material, familiarizing myself with the intricacies of quantum machine learning, and preparing for the interview process.

I submitted my application through the provided link, and as expected, it didn't take long for Dr. Roth's team to respond. They were impressed with my credentials and invited me for an interview. The speed of their response was a testament to the meticulous planning of the Astra team.

The days leading up to the interview in Houston were fraught with anxiety and confusion. The possibility of not being selected for the role lingered heavily in my mind. If I failed, the Astra team would surely deem me useless and possibly enact their deadly plan. Yet, success in the interview carried its own set of risks. Either outcome seemed to lead me closer to the edge of a precipice.

As a machine learning programmer, I had a firm grasp on the technical aspects required for the role. During the interview with the four officials, I answered most of their questions confidently, though a few responses were less certain. The outcome of the interview felt uncertain, balanced on a knife-edge between success and failure. This uncertainty only amplified my worries about the consequences of each potential outcome.

After the interview, they instructed me to stay in Houston overnight for the results. That night, my mind was a tumult of fear and anticipation. The familiar, ominous feeling of death loomed over me again. To cope, I resorted to controlling my thoughts, limiting my contemplations to moments under the shower, the only place where I felt somewhat safe from the prying influence of the nanochip.

The next day, I received a call on a new mobile phone I had acquired with my old number, the one I had previously discarded in the water. They informed me that I had been selected for the position and instructed me to undergo a medical examination at a designated hospital. The medical test was a routine procedure, but it felt like another step deeper into an inescapable web.

After the medical exam, I returned to New York by plane, a city filled with memories and emotions that now seemed distant under the shadow of my current predicament. The medical tests were clear, and now the only hurdle remaining was the background check confirmation.

For the following week, I confined myself to my apartment in New York, barely stepping outside. The isolation and the continuous monitoring of my thoughts by the Astra team through the nanochip started to take a toll on me. The lack of contact with the man in black, who had previously guided me through my dreams, left me feeling even more alone and vulnerable.

The depression of my impending death, a feeling I had become sickeningly familiar with, resurfaced. The uncertainty of what lay ahead, coupled with the constant surveillance and the control exerted over me, created an oppressive atmosphere that was hard to shake off. Each day was a struggle, filled with a sense of dread and helplessness.

Despite these challenges, I knew I had to maintain my composure and continue to play the role the Astra team expected of me. The stakes were too high, and any sign of rebellion or despair could trigger a fatal response. My thoughts were not entirely my own anymore, but I held onto the hope that there might still be a way to turn the situation around, to outsmart the Astra team and protect Earth from their sinister plans. The future was uncertain, but I was determined to face whatever challenges lay ahead.

After a week of anxious waiting, I finally received the offer letter from Dr. Roth's company, Spectra, for the position of Quantum Machine Learning Engineer. The sense of déjà vu was palpable as I left New York once again, my emotions a complex mix of fear, resignation, and a faint glimmer of hope. The city, which had once been a beacon of dreams and opportunities, now seemed to be a recurring backdrop to the various chapters of my ordeal.

The Astra team had skillfully altered my hospital reports, ensuring that my background check by Spectra would raise no suspicions. As I departed New York, memories of my last departure—filled with the dread of impending death from cancer—played in my mind. This time, the circumstances were different, yet the underlying fear of death and manipulation was eerily similar.

Arriving in Houston, I was greeted by the impressive twelve-story building of Prisma, Spectra's headquarters, located in the heart of downtown. The building's modern architecture and bustling environment were a stark contrast to the internal turmoil I was experiencing. My initial training at Prisma began immediately, led by an energetic and enthusiastic instructor. Despite the engaging nature of the training, I found it hard to focus, my thoughts constantly drifting to the Astra team's plan and the absence of any guidance from the man in black.

The lack of contact from both the Astra team and the man in black left me in a state of heightened anxiety. The man in black, who had previously appeared in my dreams, offering guidance and insight, was now conspicuously absent, leaving me to navigate this precarious situation on my own.

The 15-day training period at Prisma's headquarters was a mix of tedious sessions and overwhelming information. Although the content was closely related to my expertise in machine learning, my mind was preoccupied with the bigger picture—the role I was being forced to play in an alien plot and the potential consequences of my actions.

Houston, unlike New York, did not hold any personal attachments for me, and I found myself disliking the city. I barely ventured outside of my apartment, provided by Spectra, located near the office. The city's unfamiliarity only added to my sense of isolation and disconnection from my previous life.

As the days passed, I felt myself slipping into depression again, haunted by the realization of my mind's enslavement and the ever-present threat of death. Looking out of the window of my apartment, the world outside seemed distant and unrelatable. The reality of my situation—a pawn in a cosmic game, controlled by an advanced alien civilization—was a constant source of distress.

One evening, exhausted and overwhelmed, I fell asleep in my suit and boots, the day's training still fresh in my mind.

As I drifted into an uneasy sleep, plagued by the complexities of my situation, the familiar figure of the man in black finally reappeared in my dreamscape. His presence, which had become a source of guidance and insight in this convoluted journey, brought a mixture of relief and apprehension.

He began by explaining the difficulties he had encountered in trying to reach my mind, suggesting that the security protocols of the nanochip had likely been enhanced. His suggestion to take tranquilizers to facilitate deeper sleep was pragmatic; it would lower my mental barriers, making it easier for him to penetrate the intricate defenses woven around my consciousness by the chip. I understood the risks involved in taking tranquilizers regularly but also recognized the necessity of maintaining this line of communication.

The man in black then shared a glimmer of hope amidst the looming darkness. He was working on a plan to hack into my mind and disconnect the nanochip from the alien AGI (Artificial General Intelligence) application that controlled it. His determination to find a solution was evident, reflecting his commitment to counter the plans of his own civilization for the sake of Earth's safety.

He elaborated on the technical challenges he faced. Disconnecting the nanochip was a task of immense complexity, requiring precision and a deep understanding of both human neural networks and the alien technology that had been imposed upon me. It was a delicate operation that needed to be executed flawlessly to avoid causing irreparable damage to my brain or triggering any fail-safes that might have been programmed into the chip.

The man in black's plan was not just a technical feat; it was a race against time. The Astra team could initiate their agenda at any moment, and once set in motion, it would be nearly impossible to stop. The stakes were high, and the margin for error was virtually non-existent.

As he spoke, his voice was calm but underscored with a sense of urgency. He implored me to trust him and to follow his instructions closely. The tranquilizers were a crucial part of the plan, a necessary step to weaken the chip's defenses and allow him to access and manipulate its connections.

As the dream progressed, the man in black shared more about his motivations. He revealed a sense of responsibility and a deep-seated belief that the destruction of human civilization was an unacceptable outcome. His dissent from his people's plans was driven by a moral compass that transcended interstellar boundaries.

Waking up from the dream, I felt a renewed sense of purpose and a slight easing of the despair that had gripped me. The man in black's plan offered a ray of hope in a seemingly hopeless situation. I was ready to do whatever it took to aid his efforts, understanding that the success of this plan could mean the salvation of humanity and my liberation from the invisible shackles that bound me.

The following day marked a significant shift in my role at Spectra. I was escorted to their research lab, a high-tech facility on the outskirts of Houston, dedicated to the study of wormholes. The journey to the lab was an experience in itself, characterized by stringent security measures that underscored the importance and secrecy of the work being conducted there.

Upon arrival, I was struck by the sheer scale and sophistication of the lab. It was a state-of-the-art facility, equipped with advanced technology that seemed almost futuristic. The presence of personnel in military uniforms was a clear indicator of the collaboration between Spectra and defense agencies. This partnership, likely involving the Pentagon and possibly other government entities, hinted at the national significance of the research being conducted.

As I began my assignment, the guidance provided by the Astra team proved invaluable. Their detailed knowledge of quantum machine learning allowed me to showcase expertise beyond the expectations of my role. My performance did not go unnoticed, and within a week, I had caught the attention of the project manager. My ability to offer insights and solutions that were 'out of the box' set me apart from my colleagues, aligning perfectly with the Astra team's plan to make me stand out.

This rapid ascent in the project team's esteem was part of a calculated strategy to get closer to Dr. Alexander Roth, the visionary behind Spectra. The project manager, impressed with my contributions, expressed a desire to introduce me to Dr. Roth. This development was a critical step in the Astra team's plan, positioning me within the inner circle of the wormhole research project.

Each day at the lab was a balancing act. I was acutely aware that my every move was being monitored not just by the facility's security but also by the nanochip implanted in my brain. I had to tread carefully, maintaining the facade of a dedicated and brilliant engineer while secretly harboring the knowledge of the Astra team's ulterior motives.

The opportunity to meet Dr. Roth was both an honor and a daunting prospect. He was a figure of immense intellect and influence, a pioneer in fields that were reshaping humanity's understanding of the universe. To be recognized by someone of his stature was a testament to the effectiveness of the Astra team's plan, but it also brought me closer to the epicenter of a potentially dangerous and ethically complex situation.

As the day of my introduction to Dr. Roth approached, I grappled with the weight of the responsibility on my shoulders. I was not just a Spectra employee; I was a key player in a covert operation that could have far-reaching implications. The prospect of meeting Dr. Roth was not just a career milestone; it was a step closer to the heart of an interstellar plot that could determine the fate of Earth.

In my apartment, I reflected on the journey that had brought me here. From being diagnosed with terminal cancer to being thrust into a cosmic conflict, my life had taken turns that I could never have imagined. The knowledge that I was potentially a pawn in a game controlled by alien forces was a constant source of internal conflict. Yet, amidst the chaos, I clung to the hope that the man in black's plan to disconnect the nanochip might succeed, offering a chance to break free from this manipulation and protect humanity from an unseen extraterrestrial threat.

Meeting Dr. Alexander Roth was an experience that defied my expectations. Contrary to my assumption of encountering an older figure, Dr. Roth was surprisingly youthful in appearance. A Latin-American man in his forties, he possessed a vibrant energy that seemed to defy his years. His black hair, matched with sharp eyesight behind black glasses, gave him a distinguished yet approachable demeanor.

Dr. Roth greeted me with an enthusiasm that was both invigorating and intimidating. He had already been briefed by my manager about my talents, and he wasted no time in expressing his admiration for my skills. His questions were sharp, probing into my knowledge and experience, and I responded with precision and depth, thanks to the guidance I had received from the Astra team. His keen gaze seemed to analyze not just my words, but also the subtleties of my demeanor.

As we discussed my background, I shared my achievements and accolades in programming, watching as his interest visibly piqued. Dr. Roth's response was overwhelmingly positive, and he immediately expressed his desire to have me work directly under his guidance. This development was a significant leap forward in my covert mission, bringing me closer to the heart of the project.

The following day, I reported to Dr. Roth's office, where he provided a cursory overview of the project. He was careful not to reveal too many details, emphasizing the highly secretive nature of the work. The requirement to sign a confidentiality agreement was expected; it underscored the critical and sensitive nature of the project. I complied without hesitation, understanding that this was a standard protocol in such high-stakes research.

Once the formalities were completed, Dr. Roth began to unveil the project's true nature. He explained that we were working on something extraordinary, something that defied conventional understanding. The project involved applying the laws of quantum mechanics, and my role was to develop quantum machine learning solutions to aid in this endeavor.

It was then that Dr. Roth finally revealed the centerpiece of the project—the wormhole. He led me to a secure area within the lab, where I witnessed what could only be described as a marvel of science. The wormhole manifested as a circle of light, an ethereal gateway that seemed to hover in space. Dr. Roth explained that the wormhole was encrypted, and our current challenge was to find a way to enter it safely. The key to this, he believed, lay in the realm of quantum machine learning—my area of expertise.

The task assigned to me was monumental: to break the encryption of the wormhole using quantum machine learning algorithms. This endeavor was not just a test of my technical skills but also a significant step toward understanding and potentially utilizing this cosmic phenomenon.

As I absorbed the magnitude of the task ahead, I couldn't help but feel a mix of awe and apprehension. The opportunity to work on such a groundbreaking project was every scientist's dream, but I was acutely aware of the Astra team's hidden agenda and the nanochip that still controlled my actions. The wormhole, a gateway to the unknown, represented both a scientific breakthrough and a potential tool for alien ambitions.

As I left Dr. Roth's office that day, the image of the wormhole lingered in my mind. It was a symbol of human ingenuity and curiosity, but also a reminder of the fragile line between discovery and danger. My role in this project was pivotal, and I knew that the decisions I made in the coming days would have far-reaching consequences, not just for me, but for the entire human race.

The encounter with the mysterious man as I returned to my apartment that evening added another layer of complexity to my already convoluted situation. His apology and quick departure after our collision didn't escape my notice. It was too convenient, too calculated. I instinctively knew it wasn't a mere coincidence. The realization dawned on me that this was likely a maneuver by the Astra team to reestablish direct communication with me.

My suspicions were confirmed when I discovered a familiar object in my pocket—the same satellite phone that the Astra team had previously provided and then taken back. This stealthy exchange was their way of ensuring continued communication without raising suspicions. It was a clear indication of the intricate and risky game being played by both Spectra and the Astra team, each trying to monitor and control my actions for their purposes.

As I settled into my apartment, the satellite phone rang, piercing the silence of the room. The caller on the other end was a member of the Astra team. His voice was calm and measured, but there was an underlying tone of urgency. He began by acknowledging that they were aware of the close surveillance I was under from Spectra. They knew that my phone was likely tapped and that my movements were being monitored.

The Astra team member then briefed me on the importance of maintaining the facade of a diligent and committed Spectra employee. Any deviation from this persona could jeopardize not only the mission but also my life. He emphasized the need for utmost caution and discretion in every action I took, reminding me of the nanochip's presence and its capabilities to control my behavior or even end my life if deemed necessary.

The conversation then shifted to the task at hand—the mysterious object, the wormhole, that Dr. Roth had shown me. The Astra team member reiterated the critical nature of my role in manipulating the project's outcome. They needed me to continue gaining Dr. Roth's trust, to access more information about the wormhole, and to eventually implant the code they had provided me. This code, supposedly harmless and only meant to disable a potential weapon, was shrouded in ambiguity and uncertainty.

As the call concluded, I was left with a renewed sense of the precariousness of my position. Caught between the Astra team's manipulations and Spectra's watchful eye, I was walking a tightrope with no safety net. The weight of the responsibility I carried was immense. The fate of the wormhole project, potentially a pivotal discovery in human history, was entangled with the hidden agenda of an alien civilization.

That night, as I lay in bed, the events of the day replayed in my mind. The encounter with the man, the covert exchange of the satellite phone, and the subsequent call from the Astra team—all were pieces of a larger puzzle that I was struggling to solve. The man in black, my mysterious guide and ally, had not appeared in my dreams for some time, leaving me to navigate this labyrinth alone.

The future was uncertain, filled with potential dangers and moral dilemmas. I knew that my actions in the coming days would have significant consequences, not just for myself but for humanity as a whole. The wormhole, a portal to the unknown, represented a beacon of scientific discovery, but it also posed an unparalleled risk if misused. In this high-stakes game of espionage and interstellar intrigue, every decision mattered, and I was at the center of it all.

In the stillness of the night, the man in black returned to my dreams, bringing with him crucial information and a daunting choice. He revealed the true nature of the code provided by the Astra team. Contrary to their claims, the code was designed to permanently shut down the wormhole under Spectra's control. This shutdown wouldn't be immediate but would occur gradually over two to three days. During this period, according to the Astra team's plan, they would ostensibly take me to Russia. However, the man in black warned that their real intention was far more sinister—they planned to force me to commit suicide, likely by jumping from the 9th floor of my apartment.

The revelation was chilling, yet it was accompanied by an even more significant disclosure. The man in black presented an alternative plan, a daring and self-sacrificial strategy that could potentially save Earth from the Tera system's influence. He explained that by modifying the Astra team's code, I could close not just the one wormhole under Spectra's control but all eight wormholes worldwide through which the Tera system's agents were infiltrating Earth. This action would trap the agents already on Earth and prevent others from arriving. Furthermore, it would render the existing technology for creating new wormholes ineffective, forcing them to start from scratch with a different technology.

The gravity of this decision weighed heavily on me. Implementing the man in black's modified code would undoubtedly save humanity from the clutches of the Astra team and their civilization's plans. However, it would also seal my fate. The Astra team would undoubtedly retaliate with lethal force the moment they realized what I had done.

On the other hand, if I followed through with the Astra team's original plan, my life would be spared, but I would continue to be a pawn in their schemes, potentially aiding in further operations against Earth.

The man in black continued expressing his ongoing efforts to hack into my mind and sever the connection with the nanochip. His success in this endeavor would mean my liberation from the Astra team's control, but so far, he had not been successful.

With only three days left before I was to implement the code, the pressure of the decision was immense. On one side was the chance to play a crucial role in saving Earth, a selfless act of heroism that would cost me my life. On the other was the option to preserve my life but at the cost of continued enslavement and the potential harm to humanity.

As I awoke from the dream, the weight of this impending choice loomed over me. I was caught in a conflict that spanned beyond our planet, holding the fate of humanity in my hands. The serene morning light streaming through my window stood in stark contrast to the turmoil brewing within me.

Throughout the day, I grappled with the enormity of the decision. The thought of ending my life in a defiant act to save Earth was terrifying, yet the prospect of living at the mercy of the Astra team, facilitating their malevolent plans, was equally unbearable.

As the hours passed, my resolve began to strengthen. The man in black's plan offered a glimmer of hope—not for my survival, but for the protection of Earth. The sacrifice required was monumental, but the stakes were higher than my individual life. It was a chance to thwart the plans of a civilization that sought to dominate and potentially destroy ours.

The decision was made. I would modify the code as instructed by the man in black, closing all the wormholes and safeguarding Earth from further incursions. The risk to my life was a price I was willing to pay for the greater good of humanity.

As night fell, I prepared myself mentally and emotionally for what was to come. The next three days would be critical, and I was determined to see this through, no matter the cost. The fate of our world depended on it, and I was ready to make the ultimate sacrifice.

As I delved deeper into my work at the Spectra office, my mind was constantly preoccupied with the daunting task ahead. The evenings brought a mixture of dread and anticipation as I awaited the nightly visits from the man in black in my dreams. His latest revelation brought a wave of relief mixed with a new set of challenges.

He informed me that he had successfully interrupted the connection between my mind and the nanochip for a brief period of five minutes. During this window, he managed to disconnect the chip from the Astra team's AGI application. This development was a significant breakthrough, offering a chance at freedom from their control.

He instructed me to implement the modified code that would shut down all eight wormholes at exactly 2:00 PM. Concurrently, he would attempt to sever my connection to the nanochip permanently. Once the code was in place, I was to disclose everything to Dr. Roth—the entire plot of the Astra team, their plans for Earth, and my role in their scheme. Revealing this information to Dr. Roth was critical. His understanding and support would be vital in the aftermath of shutting down the wormholes.

The man in black then outlined a daring escape plan. After disclosing everything to Dr. Roth, I was to make a swift departure toward Bisbee, Arizona. Bisbee's outskirts were known for a natural high-power electromagnetic field, which could potentially render the nanochip ineffective.

However, reaching Bisbee from Houston would be an arduous journey, requiring at least 18 hours of driving.

The man in black assured me that he would strive to keep the chip disconnected during this time. But he warned that the Astra team might resort to physical means to stop me once they realized their control over me was waning. The road to Bisbee would be perilous, potentially lined with hazards and Astra agents equipped with advanced and lethal weaponry.

Realizing the gravity of the situation, I understood that I would need a protective escort—a squad of armed personnel to accompany me on this hazardous journey. The success of reaching Bisbee and the subsequent neutralization of the nanochip hinged on this crucial aspect.

As the day of the operation drew closer, I prepared myself for the sequence of events that would unfold. The task of inputting the code at the precise time, followed by the revelation to Dr. Roth, and the perilous journey to Bisbee, was a meticulously orchestrated plan with little margin for error.

Every passing moment was tinged with a sense of impending action, a countdown to a pivotal moment that could alter the course of human history. The responsibility I bore was immense, the stakes higher than ever. The thought of being free from the Astra team's control was a beacon of hope, but the dangers that lay ahead were daunting.

The morning of the operation, I woke up with a resolve steeled by the enormity of the task at hand. I was ready to play my part in this high-stakes game of cosmic intrigue. My actions in the next few hours would determine not just my fate but the fate of humanity. It was a burden I was ready to bear, a sacrifice I was willing to make for the greater good. As I left for the office that day, I carried with me a sense of purpose, ready to face whatever challenges lay ahead.

At precisely 2:00 PM, as planned, I executed the most critical task of my life: implanting the code into Spectra's system, a code that would cease the operation of all the wormholes. Immediately afterward, I rushed to Dr. Alexander Roth's office, determined to reveal everything. The urgency of the situation was paramount, but I was halted by a security officer. My insistence and the resulting commotion attracted the attention of my project manager, who, sensing the severity, facilitated my entry into Dr. Roth's meeting room.

Once inside, I demanded a private audience with Dr. Roth. The urgency in my voice and demeanor was enough to convince him to step aside with me. Outside, security officials gathered, sensing the unusual nature of the situation. My fear escalated, worrying whether the man in black had succeeded in disconnecting the nanochip. If he hadn't, my life could end abruptly at any moment.

Alone with Dr. Roth, I quickly divulged everything—the Astra team, their plans, the wormholes, and my coerced role in their scheme. Dr. Roth's initial disbelief gradually gave way to a realization of the gravity of the situation. Understanding the imminent danger, he acted swiftly, contacting the U. S. President to explain the unfolding events.

Soon, a helicopter arrived on the rooftop of the Spectra building, accompanied by a U. S. Army escort. Amidst this whirlwind, I remembered to retrieve my mobile phone from the security desk. As I turned it on, it immediately rang. It was Ava, her voice a mix of anger, confusion, and heartache. She spoke of Ethan telling her everything and her visit to the hospital, where she learned of my miraculous recovery. Ava's words were laced with pain and longing, and I could sense her tears through the phone.

Caught in a maelstrom of emotions, I was overwhelmed. I reassured Ava that I was in an emergency situation but promised to return to New York as soon as possible. My promise felt hollow, overshadowed by the uncertainty of my survival and the looming threat of death if the man in black's plan failed.

I boarded the helicopter, which swiftly ascended into the sky, heading toward Bisbee. As Houston's cityscape shrank beneath me, my thoughts were with Ava. The love we shared, the pain of separation, and the possibility of never seeing her again weighed heavily on my heart. Yet, amidst this emotional turmoil, there was a sense of accomplishment. I had played my part in potentially saving humanity from an unseen extraterrestrial threat.

The flight to Bisbee was a journey of introspection. As the helicopter cut through the air, I pondered over the events that had led me to this moment. From facing death due to cancer, to being entangled in an interstellar conflict, and now, flying toward an uncertain fate—it was a surreal trajectory that defied belief.

Looking down at the world below, I felt a sense of peace. Regardless of what awaited me in Bisbee, I had fulfilled my duty. The wormholes would soon cease to operate, and the Earth would be safe from the Astra team's machinations. The sacrifice and risks involved were immense, but the preservation of humanity was worth every bit.

As the helicopter neared Bisbee, the natural electromagnetic field that would hopefully neutralize the nanochip, I braced myself for what was to come. The future was uncertain, but I was ready to face it. I had done my part in this cosmic battle, and now, it was time to confront my destiny, whatever it may hold.